"Where's Fee

Stella's eyes poppe e
now-empty front se

"She's untying the toboggan."

"My saucer," the little girl said as he unfastened
her from her seat.

"It's in the back." He lifted Stella out and walked
her to the other side of the SUV, stopping to get
her sled out.

"All set," Fiona said.

He leaned the saucer against the SUV and lifted
down the toboggan. "Who wants a ride?"

"Me, me." Stella hopped up and down before
climbing on.

"I'd better grab your saucer," he said.

"Feena carry my saucer," Stella said.

Fiona's face brightened so that it outshone
the bright afternoon sun on the sparkling snow.
"I can do that."

"Teamwork. I like that," Marc said, passing the
saucer to Fiona.

"Teamwork," Stella echoed.

Marc walked with Fiona and Stella toward the low
rectangular building where they were all meeting
in the snack area. They could be a team—a team
of friends. Yeah. He and Fiona could be friends.

Jean C. Gordon's writing is a natural extension of her love of reading. From that day in first grade when she realized *t-h-e* was the word *the*, she's been reading everything she can put her hands on. Jean and her college-sweetheart husband share a 175-year-old farmhouse in Upstate New York with their daughter and her family. Their son lives nearby. Contact Jean at Facebook.com/jeancgordon.author or PO Box 113, Selkirk, NY 12158.

Books by Jean C. Gordon

Love Inspired

Small-Town Sweethearts
Small-Town Dad
Small-Town Mom
Small-Town Midwife
Reuniting His Family
A Mom for His Daughter

The Donnelly Brothers

Winning the Teacher's Heart
Holiday Homecoming
The Bachelor's Sweetheart

A Mom
for His Daughter

Jean C. Gordon

HARLEQUIN® LOVE INSPIRED®

Recycling programs for this product may not exist in your area.

LOVE INSPIRED BOOKS

ISBN-13: 978-1-335-50925-3

A Mom for His Daughter

www.Harlequin.com

Printed in U.S.A.

And we know that all things work together
for good to them that love God, to them
who are the called according to His purpose.
—*Romans* 8:28

To my Love Inspired editor, Shana Asaro, for pushing me to make this story a better book.

Chapter One

Everything Marc Delacroix had always thought he wanted rode on decisions he and his business partners would make in the next few hours. And he couldn't care less.

Oh, he'd gone through the motions yesterday of meeting with Fiona Bryce, the Cornell farm-to-table consultant. He owed his partners that much. They'd been picking up the slack for him even before Cate's death. The lump that formed in his throat when he thought about his wife didn't choke off his windpipe anymore, which he guessed was progress. This Lake George restaurant launch his partners had sent him north for felt a lot like a get-yourself-together-or-sell-out proposition. He curled his lip. Maybe he should sell out.

His cell phone jolted him from his thoughts. He glanced at the caller ID. *Mom.* Just what he didn't need when he was rushing to get his daughter, Stella, dressed and to her first morning at preschool in Schroon Lake. But he couldn't ignore her. She was his mother.

"Hey, Mom. What's up? I only have a minute if I'm going to get Stella to school on time."

"But she's not quite three yet. So little for preschool," his mother protested.

While he listened to his mother's opinion on Stella and preschool for the third time, his thoughts drifted back to yesterday. Although he only had a vague idea of what Fiona's program could do, he'd forwarded her presentation with his positive recommendation to his partners. He'd been unexpectedly mesmerized by the woman—her features, her movements—and had paid more attention to her than to what she'd said.

"Marc?"

"Yes, I'm here, Mom. I was thinking about my meeting at the research farm yesterday."

"I'm glad you're taking an interest in your work again," she said.

More like an interest in my potential business consultant. But it was something. Better than the apathy that had paralyzed him for the past months.

"You know I don't mind watching Stella," his mother said. "I'm free today if you want to get some work in. I usually don't schedule any bookkeeping on Wednesdays to have a day free for errands and other things."

That was the drawback and blessing of having moved Stella from New York City to his hometown of Paradox Lake in the Adirondack Mountains. Lots of people always ready to help. Mom with her offers to take care of Stella. His twin sister pressing him to socialize, meet new people—Fiona, her coworker at the Cornell Research Farm in Willsboro, popped into his mind again—and encouraging him to get started on La Table Frais, his restaurant project.

Cradling the phone between his ear and shoulder, Marc picked up Stella's shoes, slipped them on her feet and pressed the Velcro fasteners. He was inclined to agree with his mother, but his youngest sister, Renee, a child sociologist, had convinced him that being with children her age would help get Stella up to speed with the age-appropriate behavior she'd fallen behind on.

"It's a play group for two- and three-year-olds. And Andie will be there." His older sister was one of the teachers at The Kids Place, the childcare center at Hazardtown Community Church, where he and his family attended services.

"Stella. Red," Stella said, pointing at her belly and her red T-shirt in a basket of clothes he had folded, ready to put away.

"Okay." Marc hoped he wasn't pushing Stella too hard. Her speech development had stalled since Cate died. But referring to herself in a baby-like third person was something new he'd noticed since they'd moved here last month.

"Pardon?" his mother said.

Stella scampered over to the basket, pulled off the shirt he'd put on her and worked at putting on the red one.

"Stella wanted to wear her red shirt instead of the one I put on her."

He could imagine the expression on his mother's face about letting Stella have her way. Marc grabbed his phone from his shoulder. But the counselor they'd seen downstate after Cate's death had said to choose his battles with Stella, and he wasn't about to do anything to set her off before he even got her to The Kids Place.

"I don't want to upset her, Mom. She had a meltdown yesterday at the grocery store. Someone Stella didn't know said hello to her, and Stella went ballistic. You know how reluctant she can be about talking to new people." Or anyone other than him—even his family.

"That's what I mean. Stella may need more time with family to adjust to her new home. School's off today for a teacher's workday or something. I could have Robbie come and play with her."

Yeah. A playdate with his toddler cousin wasn't likely to be at the top of seven-year-old Robbie's wish list.

"I need to go, Mom. I've got work to do after I drop off Stella." He strained to hide the catch in his voice on *work*. How many times had he said that to Cate, to Stella, thinking there would be time later? Then Cate was dying, and there were no more laters.

"Daddy!"

He turned. Stella had her arm through the head of the shirt.

"And Stella needs help with her shirt."

"Okay, and as I said, if you want to go work on the restaurant this afternoon, I'll be here for Stella."

"Thanks, Mom." But *he* was the one who ought to be there for his daughter. "I'll let you know. Bye." He turned to Stella. "Hang on, sweetpea. I'll give you a hand." He pulled her arm out of the head hole, and she slipped her arms in the sleeves.

"Stella do it."

"Yep. Good job." Edginess fired through his veins. He could only hope he was doing as well.

"Church. Singing," Stella said a few minutes later when he pulled into the church parking lot and stopped in a space near the church hall.

Marc hopped out and released Stella from her car seat. "I don't know about singing today."

His wife's beautiful voice singing "On Eagles' Wings" with their church choir floated through his head. Stella had loved Cate's singing; so much so that he'd avoided taking Stella to church after Cate's death for fear the music would set Stella off. Regret squeezed his chest. But he couldn't avoid church services here. Nor did he want to. And Stella had been fine when they'd attended church with his parents last week.

The corners of Stella's mouth turned down.

"But we'll see. There might be singing." He lifted her from the car.

"Stella walk."

He set her down and took her hand. "Okay." Slowly, they made their way to the hall door. Marc opened it.

"London Bridge is falling down, falling down…" A group of preschoolers was playing London Bridge in the hall.

"See, Daddy, singing."

"You're absolutely right." His heart lightened. "Let's go talk with Aunt Andie about school."

"'Kay." Stella's voice lacked the enthusiasm of a minute ago.

Andie walked over to them. He held his breath when she crouched to Stella's level.

"Hi, Stella. We're coloring our class banner." Andie pointed across the room to several kids Stella's age sitting at a table with a long sheet of white paper. "Want to help us?"

Stella looked up at him. "Daddy color?"

"Remember, Daddy has to work this morning." He planned on talking with his partners. "You can color with Aunt Andie." The counselor had told Marc that the little girl might feel more secure with him telling her what to do, rather than asking—at least for a while.

Stella stared at him silently for so long his heart stopped. Then she nodded and took Andie's hand.

"She'll be fine," Andie said.

"Right." He resisted looking back at Stella as he left

the hall. Stella knew Andie. Andie was great with kids of all ages, and she had his number if there was any problem.

Marc dragged his feet walking out to the car. He needed to occupy his mind with something more than concerns about Stella. That fixation wasn't good for her or him. He'd taken his first reluctant step yesterday toward an opportunity he would have jumped at in a New York minute two years ago. Marc wanted that excitement back. For too long, he'd been plodding through life placing one foot in front of the other.

He made his decision. He needed to get in the race again, call Fiona and let her know she could write up a consulting contract for La Table Frais. His partners would probably celebrate his taking the initiative to make the decision, rather than waiting for their approval.

Sitting in the driver's seat, he thumbed to the Cornell Research Farm's number on his phone, picturing Fiona, her coppery curls, wide-set hazel eyes and vivacious mannerisms. She was a stunning woman, and the first woman he'd noticed since Cate had died.

If he were honest with himself, that scared him. He closed his eyes. His main focus still had to be Stella, but to be what his daughter needed, maybe he needed something for himself.

He didn't have to throw himself into the new restaurant 24/7 as he had with his work in New York. And having an adult relationship, a nonpressure business relationship that had nothing to do with his daughter, might give him a balance between family and work.

Fiona adjusted and readjusted the blinds on the small window in her work cubicle to block the glare from the afternoon sun and checked her email—again. Nothing from Marc Delacroix. She knew he'd received the copy of her presentation she'd sent him. She had the return receipt email. Had he shared it with his partners? It wasn't a make-or-break situation, but getting Marc and his partners in New York City involved in her new program would be a great start toward making the program—and her job—secure.

She minimized her email. Marc had seemed interested in what she'd presented. Although he hadn't taken many notes and had asked only a few questions, he'd been intent on the presentation, focused on her.

She pictured Marc, his dark, thickly lashed eyes, the all-masculine planes of his face. Claire hadn't been exaggerating with her clichéd tall, dark and handsome description of her twin. In fact, she may have been underplaying his attractiveness.

Fiona blinked away the picture. This was work. Although from the glowing report Claire had given of her brother's experience, his business connections in New York City *and* his personal attributes, Fiona couldn't help but think there was more behind Claire's push to get them together than simply business. Especially given Claire's emphasis on how much she thought Marc and Fiona had in common—essentially their dedication to their work and interest in promoting locally produced food. Neither was anything to build a personal relationship on.

Fiona put a halt to the odd direction her thoughts had taken. If Claire knew more about her, she wouldn't have given a thought to putting her and Marc together. But they had only met recently, new coworkers.

Fiona rubbed the side of the mouse. She was trying to put the unhappy parts of her past behind her by taking the position here, near Ticonderoga. The place where she'd had an intact family—at least for a while. The only place she remembered being truly happy. She hoped to find the peace she'd been searching for most of her life, and closure for her younger sister Mairi's senseless death. She refused to believe all her efforts to hold her family together had been in vain, despite the fact that the sister she'd mostly raised had turned to drugs as their mother had.

Fiona's desk phone rang.

"Hey, Fiona, you have a delivery you need to sign for," the staffer at the front desk said.

"I'll be right out." As she walked to the front desk, Fiona searched her memory for anything she'd ordered that she'd have to sign for and came up blank.

"I'm Fiona Bryce. You have something for me?"

"Fiona C. Bryce?" the deliverer asked.

"Yes." How many Fiona Bryces could there be here? "Do you need ID?" She tapped her employer badge hanging from the lanyard around her neck.

The man glanced at it. "That's fine. Please sign here." He handed her a clipboard and pointed to a line.

Fiona signed and accepted the cardboard envelope. The return address was the attorney in Glens Falls she'd hired to help her settle Mairi's estate, what little there had been of it anyway. Her heart thumped. That had all been taken care of nearly two years ago. She hadn't thought to give him her new address or phone number. He must have tracked her online to the Willsboro farm.

On her way back to her cubicle, Fiona tore open the cardboard. Settling in the chair behind her desk, she pulled out the attorney's letter and read it.

"...the new owners of the cabin where your sister died were refinishing a desk there as part of renovations to rent it and found the enclosed stamped envelope addressed to you caught behind one of the drawers. They knew about your sister, so they passed the letter on to the local authorities. The chief of police, my brother-in-law, forwarded it to me, thinking I'd have your address. All I could find was the address of your business."

Fiona's heart slammed against her chest as she reached inside the cardboard mailer and withdrew a white business envelope with her name and the address of the USDA experimental farm in Guam where she'd been working when Mairi died. It was in Mairi's handwriting, scribbled but definitely Mairi's. Fiona drew deep inside herself for strength that was beyond her own.

Dear Lord, be with me now.

She carefully slid her finger under the flap and ripped through it with a sharp jerk. Closing her eyes and doing her best to take a cleansing breath, she unfolded the pages. The letter was dated the day Mairi had died.

I'm sorry I failed you, the letter read in the same scribbled handwriting as the envelope. *I'm weak like Mom. I tried to call and tell you, but I couldn't do it. I tried to take care of her like you would, but I couldn't.*

Fiona unsuccessfully tried to blink away her tears. Take care of who? She refocused on the sheet.

I love you. She's safe with the people at Precious in His Sight. I couldn't wait until you came back. Find her. I have to go now. I'm going to put this out in the mailbox. Mairi.

Fiona choked, her mind flooding with questions. *I have to go?* Did that mean Mairi had OD'd on purpose because of whatever her letter was talking about? Either before she'd written the letter or right after, and become disoriented or passed out before she could mail it? Or had she decided not to send it? Struggling to draw a breath, Fiona shuffled to the next sheet and dropped it as if it were a burning ember, her gazed fixed on the words "Fiona Elsbeth Collins, born…"

A baby? Her breath left her lungs in a sudden rush. Hand shaking, Fiona picked up the birth certificate and read the remainder of the information. Mother: Mairi A. Collins. Father: Unknown. Date of Birth: March 3. Place of birth: Town of Ticonderoga. *Mairi had a baby.*

Fiona muffled her sobs. She might never know all that happened with Mairi, why her baby was born in Ticonderoga rather than in the central New York village where she had worked as a nurse. Why Mairi had never sent this letter. But there was a precious piece of Mairi remaining in the world—a three-year-old niece. Maybe this was God's path to closure on her sister's death. The opportunity to make up for not being able to keep her family together, for her failing Mairi. All she had to do was find the little girl.

Marc pushed open the door to the church hall, still debating whether tonight was a good idea. But Claire had sounded desperate, texting that several members of the Twenty-/Thirtysomethings group had bailed on her. The group was supposed to be spending its usual Thursday night meeting time helping set up for the winter bazaar and book sale Saturday.

He'd been resisting his sister's urging to join what had been the Singles group at church, but was now made up of a mix of marrieds and singles. Marc wasn't looking to meet anyone for a romantic relationship— which his attraction to Fiona contradicted. From the disastrous months following Cate's death, he knew juggling work and being a single parent was more than enough for him to handle.

"Daddy, school," Stella said when they stepped into the hall.

Marc tensed. After refusing to take a nap at his mother's—he'd taken Mom up on her earlier offer to watch Stella this afternoon while he went down to Lake George to look at the restaurant property—Stella had zonked out on the couch right after dinner and woken up cranky. She'd still been out of sorts when they'd left the house. Maybe they should have stayed home. What if she *was* getting sick? He talked himself down. She wasn't running a temperature, had eaten a good dinner and hadn't complained about not feeling well.

He unzipped her coat and took her hat and mittens off. "Not school. Playtime with Aunt Andie's big girls, Aimee and Amelia."

"Stella big girl."

"Yes, you are." At times, he wondered if she said that because he babied her or to affirm it to herself. He scanned the room for his teenage nieces or Claire, and stopped at a tumble of red curls. *Fiona*. Did Claire's call for help have an ulterior motive? The bigger question was, did he mind if her motive had been more than getting his assistance?

"Uncle Marc!" His niece's shout drew his attention away.

She hurried over. "Hi," she said breathlessly. "We're watching the kids in the preschool room. We're going to make snowflakes with silver and gold glitter."

"Stella help?" She looked up at him.

"Definitely. I'm sure they can use your help."

Stella smiled and walked away with his niece. That was easy. He shoved Stella's hat and mittens into his jacket pocket. A bit of him wanted to see Stella's hesitation to leave him that he'd come to expect, but most of him was relieved that Stella was becoming more comfortable with other people. His family, at least.

"You made it. I wasn't sure from your text if you would." Claire appeared beside him.

"I'm here. What do you have for me to do?"

"Table setup. You can put your coat on the table by the door with the others. And a truck full of books is coming that needs to be unloaded."

"Who else do you have to bring the tables down from upstairs?"

"Pastor Connor. Then he has an appointment. The rest of the guys bailed, as I said in my text." Claire looked around the room. "Fiona can help you set up the tables and unload the books."

Marc pinned his twin's gaze, questioning the possibility of a different type of setup. "I didn't know Fiona was a member of the group." He hadn't seen her at church service in all the time he'd been here.

"She's not, but I'm working on it as I am with you. Fiona helped her landlady, Mrs. Hamilton, the other evening, sorting items for the rummage sale."

Marc wasn't sure what that had to do with tonight.

"Mrs. Hamilton was going to supervise the work tonight, but her hip is acting up, and she asked Fiona to step in for her." Claire stopped. "What's with the face? It's like you want to avoid Fiona. Didn't your meeting yesterday go well?"

"It went well enough." What *was* with him was that he wanted to spend time with Fiona, and that put him on edge. Fiona belonged in the business part of his life, not the social one. He raked his hand through his hair. He didn't have a social life anyway. Not anymore.

* * *

Fiona stopped dead, her gaze glued to the red-haired toddler holding Marc's hand. The copper curls. Her profile. The little girl's button nose. She looked so much like a photo Fiona had at home of Mairi as a toddler. Fiona's lungs burned, reminding her to take a breath.

It couldn't be. Claire hadn't said anything about her niece, Stella, being adopted. Fiona pushed her hair back from her face. Her emotions were worn raw from reading and rereading her sister's letter, trying to fully understand. She'd hoped busying herself with the bazaar setup would give her mind and emotions a rest for a few hours. Fiona watched the toddler walk out of the room with a dark-haired teenager. She couldn't let her desires distort reality. She'd only be setting herself up for disappointment again.

Fiona started when Claire touched her shoulder.

"I didn't mean to startle you," her friend said. "Are you okay? You're so pale."

Fiona waved her off. "I'm fine." As fine as she could manage at the moment.

"Marc and Pastor Connor are bringing the tables down from upstairs. Give them a few minutes and they should be ready to help you arrange them."

"Okay." Fiona waited until Claire had taken a few steps in the opposite direction and fled to the ladies' room. She splashed water on her face and stared. The smattering of freckles across her nose popped against her still pale skin. She had to get a grip on herself, work out a systematic plan for finding her niece. Otherwise, she'd be seeing Mairi in every red-haired little girl she saw on the street, in the store…

Fiona returned to the hall and approached Marc and

a man she assumed was Pastor Connor, who were adding a table to a stack leaning against the wall.

"Hi, I'm Fiona Bryce. You must be Pastor Connor."

"Yes. Nice to meet you. I read about your program at the Research Farm."

"Speaking of which," Marc said, "did you get my voice mail?"

"No, sorry. I didn't check it. I had meetings all morning and left the office early." After reading Mairi's letter, she couldn't concentrate on work, so she'd gone home to research and contact Precious in His Sight and to rehash where she'd gone wrong with Mairi. She'd tried to give her the support and direction their parents hadn't given them.

"Go ahead and write up a contract proposal for La Table Frais," Marc said.

"Great. I'll get to work on it tomorrow." She tried to force the enthusiasm she should be feeling for her program's first major client. "Your partners agreed, then?"

"They will." Marc's dark eyes sparkled.

This Marc jibed more with the description his sister had given Fiona of a man who could have won their high school's most-likely-to-succeed award when he was in kindergarten than the quiet, intent man she'd met with at the farm.

"I've got to get ready for my meeting," Pastor Connor interrupted, tilting his head toward the outer hall and his office. "You two should be able to handle setting up without me."

"Where do you want the tables?" Marc asked as Connor walked away.

Fiona showed Marc the diagram Mrs. Hamilton had given her, unsettled by the awareness of him close beside her, looking over her shoulder at the paper she held. *Sheesh!* She'd stood next to attractive men before. Mairi's letter had her nerves totally on edge about everything.

"Simple enough," he said, and they went to work.

As Fiona watched Marc snap the legs of the last table into place and tip it upright, an elderly woman with a cane stepped into the hall from the parking lot and looked around.

"Can I help you?" Fiona asked.

"I have books to donate. I talked with Betty Hamilton."

"Yes, we're expecting you. Tell us which vehicle and we'll unload. You can wait in here where it's warm."

"The gray SUV with the Essex County Farm Co-op sticker on the back window. The hatch is unlocked."

Marc and Fiona grabbed their coats from the pile on the table by the door and headed out. Fiona quickly spotted the woman's SUV. She pointed at the decal on the back window and touched her foot to the hatch opener. "It's short notice, but I didn't think of it yesterday. When we're done unloading, remind me to talk with you about the co-op organizational meeting tomorrow morning."

"Sure. Let's get started," Marc said, and she wondered if he was in a hurry to be done. Or was that just her perception because she wasn't in any hurry? She traced his profile with her gaze as he leaned into the SUV. He probably wanted to get back to his daughter, and she had nothing else to do this evening except go back to her empty apartment and Mairi's letter.

He lifted one of the smaller boxes and passed it to Fiona. Her hand brushed his as she took it from him. The warmth of the contact left an imprint on her in the cold evening air.

"Go ahead and take your box inside," he said before

reaching for another one. "If we alternate, we won't be bumping into each other."

"Good idea." She gripped the box tighter and headed back to the hall. Had he felt something, too, when their hands had brushed? She glanced over her shoulder. He'd stacked two boxes to carry in, confirming her thought that he wanted to be done.

"Only two left," Fiona said a few minutes later, placing a box on the table next to the two Marc had brought in.

"I'll get them," he said.

"And I'll come and close the hatch."

He opened the outside door, and she brushed by him.

"About the Farm Co-op meeting I mentioned. You might want to come and meet some of your potential food suppliers. I can tell you about it while we walk. I understand if you're in a hurry to get your daughter home." Fiona paused. "I saw her come in with you. She's a cutie."

"I have time," he said.

"She must take after her mother, the red hair." Fiona absently touched her own hair, then jerked her hand away. Why was she going on about his daughter and not the meeting? Because all she could think about was her unanswered questions about her sister and her niece.

His eyes narrowed. "I can't really say. She's adopted."

Fiona stumbled, catching herself on the back of the car they were passing. Stella was adopted? Her heart leaped to her throat. From what she'd found out about Precious in His Sight, although the adoption agency was based near here in Glens Falls, it served Christian families throughout New York state.

Fiona pressed her palm to her throat as the realization hit her. Stella could be her niece.

Chapter Two

The north wind blew the icy snow in Fiona's face as she dashed from her car to the Ticonderoga Birthing Center. She was here in search of answers to questions about her sister. She hadn't gotten any answers about Stella last night. Before Fiona had been able to form coherent words to ask Marc about the little girl's adoption, a teen had come racing out to the parking lot to get him because Stella was crying and wouldn't stop. And the callback Fiona had received this morning to the voice mail she'd left with Precious in His Sight yesterday was what she'd expected. The adoption records for Mairi's daughter were sealed.

Maybe she'd learn something about Mairi today from the birthing center's midwife, Autumn Hanlon, or her ob-gyn husband, Jon. They apparently were the only game in town when it came to delivering babies. The next closest facility was in Vermont, and there were two others, each an hour away, in Saranac Lake and Glens Falls. But Mairi's baby's birth certificate said the Town of Ticonderoga.

Fiona stomped the snow off her boots on the entryway mat. But what if Mairi had given birth by herself?

She shuddered at the thought of her little sister giving birth all alone in the remote cabin where her body had been found. And her date of death was almost four weeks after the baby's birth date.

She removed her hat and gloves. Where had Mairi and the baby been during that time? Mairi had rented the cabin the day before her death, alone as far as the police could tell, giving a false name and paying cash for her stay. Of course, Mairi had known all about flying under the radar from their mother.

Fiona crossed the entryway and pulled open the glass door to the center at exactly two o'clock, fifteen minutes ahead of her appointment time. When she'd called the birthing center yesterday afternoon, she'd been thankful Autumn had a cancellation in her schedule and an appointment had been available today. Learning anything about Mairi, what she'd gone through, what she could have been thinking, would help Fiona fill the void inside her.

She walked to the reception window. "Fiona Bryce. I have an appointment to see Autumn Hanlon at two fifteen."

The appointment clerk pressed a key on her computer and handed Fiona some forms. While she waited to be called, Fiona sat in the waiting area, tapping the clipboard with the uncompleted forms against her leg and thinking about Stella and Marc. Marc Delacroix was an attractive, interesting man. An attractive, interesting man who was a business associate and could be her niece's adoptive father.

"Fiona Bryce."

Fiona gripped the clipboard, rose and followed the nurse to the exam room. A few minutes later, the midwife knocked on the door and stepped into the room.

"Hi, I'm Autumn Hanlon."

"Hi," Fiona answered, pressing her hand to her stomach to stop the sudden flutter of guilt about approaching the woman under the guise of being a patient.

Autumn glanced at the clipboard with the blank forms and frowned. "What brings you in?"

Fiona cleared her throat. "I'm looking for information. I believe you or your husband delivered my sister, well, half-sister's baby. Her name was Mairi Collins."

"I can't give you any information without your sister's permission. HIPPA regulation," Autumn said.

Fiona blinked. "I know the HIPPA rules. But Mairi is dead." Fiona took a certified copy of her sister's death certificate and two other documents out of her bag and handed them to Autumn. "I was the executor of her estate and had her medical power of attorney."

"I'm sorry to hear about your sister." Autumn glanced at the papers. "I remember her. We don't have that many births a year, and she was unusual in that she'd gotten her prenatal care elsewhere."

"Thank you," Fiona said. "She OD'd at a summer cabin not too far from here."

Autumn's eyes widened. "That was your sister? The local news gave a different name."

"She used a fake name. It took the police a while to actually ID her and contact me."

"Again, I'm so sorry." Autumn examined the document Fiona had given her. "Yes, I helped your sister birth her daughter." The midwife looked as if she wanted to bite her tongue.

"I know it was a baby girl. Her original birth certificate recently came into my possession. That's how I learned the baby was born in Ticonderoga and deduced she was probably born here."

Autumn nodded.

Fiona squeezed her hands in her lap. "Were there any signs of drug use, that my sister was shooting heroine?"

"No. The baby was born healthy, and your sister tested negative."

"About the baby. Mairi gave her up for adoption?"

"Yes, but not right away." Autumn hesitated. "About a month after the birth, your sister returned with the baby and said she wanted to give her up for adoption. I talked with her for quite a while. From her demeanor and things she said, I suspected postpartum depression. I suggested an overnight admission so we could observe her and she could be sure adoption was what she wanted to do. Your sister was adamant about not staying. She started to fill out the papers, signed them and excused herself to use the restroom. She never returned. We released the baby to the adoption agency she'd chosen."

"Precious in His Sight," Fiona said.

Autumn tilted her head in question.

"That information was with the birth certificate. Do you think Mairi could have committed suicide because of the postpartum depression?" Fiona stared at her hands. "Our mother was an addict. Overdoses were something we were both familiar with."

"It's possible."

The signs that Mairi had chosen drugs due to postpartum depression with the objective of suicide lifted one gray cloud of guilt. But it didn't answer why Mairi hadn't confided in her. Fiona would have given up her job and come back to the States if Mairi had said she needed her. Fiona closed her eyes. Hadn't she known that?

"Are you all right?" Autumn asked.

"As all right as I can be. One more thing. I'd like a copy of Mairi's medical records."

"Of course. I can have the records ready for you to pick up after noon tomorrow."

"Thank you. I'll stop in on my lunch break."

Fiona left in an emotional fog, settled her bill and almost physically ran into Marc and Stella in the building entryway.

"Hi," Marc said.

"What are you doing here?" she blurted, failing in her attempt to pull herself together.

"Seeing the pediatrician who's here at the center a couple of times a week."

Her cheeks heated. "Is Stella all right?"

Fiona's gaze dropped from his face to the little girl wrapped around his leg, finger stuck in her mouth. An arrow of pain struck her heart. Last evening when she'd seen Stella with Marc, she'd allowed that it could have been her imagination fired by her renewed grief over her sister's death. But it wasn't. Stella was a mini Mairi.

"It's her regular wellness appointment."

"Ah, does that mean someone has a birthday soon?" Fiona smiled at Stella, who tightened her grip on Marc.

"Not until March third, but I wanted to get her set up with a doctor here."

Marc's words after *March third*, the birth date of Mairi's daughter, were more a hum in Fiona's ears than actual words. "What agency did you and your wife use to adopt Stella?" Fiona blurted. But even before he answered, the truth rang in her like a bell, with the memory of her sister's final words: *Find her.*

Marc stared at Fiona, and then over her shoulder at the door to the Birthing Center, Autumn and Jon's practice. Bittersweet remembrances of Cate and all the tests to determine why they couldn't conceive rolled over him.

Fiona shuffled her feet and twisted the strap on her purse. "I was wondering." Her words rushed out. "For one of my classmates from grad school who I keep in touch with. I assume you used a downstate agency."

She looked at him with an eager expression that made him wonder if the information really was for a friend. "No, we used Precious in His Sight, a private Christian agency in Glens Falls. It serves all of New York state." He glanced at Stella and experienced the awe and gratitude he still got just knowing she was his. "Tell your friend I highly recommend them."

"Daddy." Stella tugged at his hand. "Good girl prize." The pediatrician Cate had taken Stella to in New York gave her a small prize at every appointment. He had no idea if the doctor here did the same, and had explained that to Stella.

He turned back to Fiona. She was staring at his daughter with a look of longing that made him wonder if she was the one who wanted to adopt. "I'd better get Stella in for her appointment."

"Of course." Fiona pulled her gaze from Stella, concern replacing the longing on her face.

"Thanks for the information. I'll tell... I'll tell my friend, and be in touch."

He watched her walk out, assuming she meant she'd be in touch about La Table Frais.

"Daddy. Her go away. 'Pointment."

He didn't know whether Stella was making an observation about Fiona leaving or expressing a preference—not that it mattered. His relationship with Fiona was business.

A half hour later, Marc was sitting in the pediatrician's exam room with the doctor and Stella.

The doctor had finished Stella's exam. "I read the medical records from Stella's previous doctor. She's always been in the lower third of children her age in height and weight. Am I correct in assuming her mother is petite?"

He leaned forward on the arms of the chair. "I don't really know. Stella is adopted."

The doctor made a note on a pad beside her. "I don't want to alarm you, but over the months since her last checkup, she's fallen into the lowest tenth. With that and the stomach upsets you said she's been experiencing, I want to refer her to a gastroenterologist at the Adirondack Medical Center. Dr. Franklin."

From the way the doctor's expression softened, the fear careening through him must have shown on his face. She looked more the grandmother she might be and less the medical professional.

"Dr. Franklin is a good man as well as physician. Great with kids. We can set up the appointment for you, or I can send a referral and you can make it yourself."

"Send the referral. I'll make the appointment." *After I talk with Autumn or Jon.* It wasn't that he didn't trust the pediatrician. But he didn't know her. He'd grown up with Autumn, gone all through school with her and knew he could trust her opinion.

"Daddy, Stella good girl?"

"Yes, you were a very good girl." He lifted her down from the examination table and looked at the doctor apologetically. "Her other pediatrician gave her what he called a good girl prize after her exams."

The doctor smiled. "It just so happens I have something for you, Stella." She handed Stella a coloring book called *Teddy Bear Goes to the Doctor's*.

"What do you say, Stella?"

The little girl beamed. "Fank you."

"You're welcome."

Marc couldn't help but compare how at ease Stella was with the doctor to the way she'd hugged his leg and tried to hide behind him the whole time he'd talked with Fiona in the entryway. Maybe she was experiencing an aversion to younger women or, as Claire had suggested, women Cate's age who had light hair like she'd had. Stella was okay around his sisters.

Marc rubbed the middle of his forehead. He didn't know why he was even concerned about Stella and Fiona together. It wasn't as if there would be many occasions for that—no matter his attraction.

The doctor typed a note into her tablet. "I'll get that referral off to the gastroenterologist. You should be set to make the appointment this afternoon."

"Thanks." He took Stella's papers and her hand and checked out.

"Let's see what we can rustle up for lunch," he said as he walked her to the car.

"Let's rustle lunch." She giggled, her full sentence capturing his heart with hope that she was making progress.

After lunch, Stella fell asleep on the couch while coloring in her new book, and he straightened up the place, waiting for his friends Autumn or Jon to return the call he'd left for them. He squatted to pick up Stella's crayons but thought better. She should pick them up. It's how Mom would do it.

His phone vibrated, and he pulled it from his back pocket. Private Caller. Probably the birthing center number. Marc swiped the screen to answer as he walked to the kitchen.

"Hello."

"Marc? It's Autumn. I got your message. What's up?"

It could be his concern about Stella and the referral, but Autumn's casual question sounded forced. He told her about Stella's exam.

"What do you know about Dr. Franklin at the medical center?"

"The best in the area, especially for children." Autumn paused. "Anything else?"

"No, that's it. I wanted a second opinion."

"Okay, then," Autumn said with what sounded oddly like relief.

But that made no sense. He pulled the slip of paper with Dr. Franklin's phone number from his wallet, but a text came in before he could dial. *Fiona*. He'd added her to his business contacts.

Hi, how did Stella's appointment go?

Marc scratched the side of his neck. He was used to his mother and sisters' friends and his business partner's wives asking him about Stella because he figured that was what women, especially mothers, talked about. Although Fiona's question wasn't any different, it prickled his spine.

Okay, he typed back.

Could we get together this evening?

Fiona was using Stella as a lead-in to getting together? He couldn't say it was the first time since Cate's death that a woman had. He slumped against the wall.

From their work together at church the other evening, he'd thought better of Fiona.

It's about Stella appeared before he could form a response. Marc pressed the i-button at the top of his screen and then the telephone icon to call Fiona. He wore off the sudden spike of adrenaline by tapping his foot while the phone rang. He didn't need this, whatever it was, on top of Stella's doctor's appointment.

Even though Fiona had expected Marc to respond, she nearly dropped the plate she was putting in the cupboard when her phone rang on the counter. She stared at his flashing caller ID and debated whether to let it ring. She'd thought he'd text back to her casual invitation to get together. Her fingers had seemed to go off on their own and added It's about Stella. She drummed her fingernails on the counter before pressing the answer button with her other thumb.

"Hello."

"This is Marc Delacroix. I got your text. Why would you need to talk with me about my daughter?"

"I'm sorry. My text was cryptic."

Fiona clearly heard the derision in the puff of breath Marc released.

"Can I start over? I have an important reason for talking with you about Stella."

"I'd like to hear it."

Fiona took a deep breath and kept her voice low. "I had wanted to say this in person. I'm almost certain Stella is my sister's child."

The phone went silent for so long, Fiona wondered if he'd hung up, except her phone showed the call was still connected.

"I'm supposed to believe that because you, practically a stranger, say so? And what's next? You're going to tell me she wants her back? No way. Your sister, if she really is Stella's birth mother, gave up her parental rights. The adoption was finalized nearly two years ago."

"My sister is dead."

"I'm sorry." Marc's voice had lost some of its edge. "But what do you want?"

Some family to love and to love me. She couldn't say that. He'd think she was unstable. "To be part of Stella's life, as her aunt, like your sisters," Fiona answered.

He ignored her answer. "Can you prove it?"

"That Stella is Mairi's daughter? I think so. I have information and documents and photos of Mairi at Stella's age." The last part sounded like she was grasping at straws. "Can we meet?"

"Not until I talk with a lawyer. Don't call me. I'll call you." His phone clicked off.

That hardly could have gone worse. She leaned on the counter. So much for the fantasy she'd concocted on the drive home after Marc had dismissed her at the birthing center. A fantasy of her becoming part of the Delacroix family, of Stella staying over at her apartment, them exploring things together as she and Mairi had. A fantasy of Marc welcoming her help with Stella so he could put in more time on his restaurant launch.

Fiona slapped the countertop. But Stella was family. The only family she had, and she was going to fight to be in her life. It's what she did, what she'd always done—fight to keep her family together.

Marc met Claire on her doorstep when she got home from work. He'd hated to drop Stella on his mom again, despite her insisting it was fine, but he needed to talk with someone away from little ears. And who got him better than his twin?

She eyed the bag from the Chinese restaurant around the corner from her apartment in Ticonderoga. "Happy Star? This must be serious."

"More than you could guess." Marc rose from his seat on the steps and followed his sister upstairs and into the kitchen.

"Get the food out, and I'll get us drinks." Claire opened the refrigerator. "I have lemonade, root beer and milk, or I can brew you a cup of coffee."

"Root beer's good." He took the plastic cartons out of the bag and placed them on the table. "How well do you know Fiona Bryce?"

Claire raised an eyebrow suggestively as she placed the drinks on the table.

"Not like that." Although the slight trip of his heart contradicted the force of his response.

"Just as a coworker. She seems nice, good at her job. We had lunch together the other day." Claire hesitated. "From something she let slip about moving a lot, I got the feeling she may have had a rough childhood. But she seems like someone I could be friends with."

He pressed his lips together. "Would you say she's honest?"

Claire opened her food container and studied the contents. "As far as I know. Why?"

Marc took a slug of his drink. His throat was suddenly parched. "She says she's Stella's aunt."

"Oh."

"Yeah. *Oh* and then some."

"Do *you* think she's telling the truth?"

For whatever reason, even without proof, he did.

"Possibly. If you've noticed, her hair is exactly like Stella's and she says she has information and documents and photos of her sister as a child that look like they could be of Stella."

"What are you going to do?"

"I'm not sure. That's why I'm talking to you, to help me decide. I called the lawyer who handled the adoption. She assured me that I'm rock solid on it."

"You think Fiona wants to challenge it?"

"I don't know. She said she only wants to be part of Stella's life as her aunt." And he'd believed her. Or wanted to believe her, anyway.

"Could she be after money?"

He hadn't thought of that. He laughed. "If so, she'll have an uphill battle with that. Everything I own is sunk into the restaurant partnership and a job that's dependent on what's currently an empty shell of a building." The sarcastic humor drained from him. "She wants to get together to talk."

"Just the two of you? Is that wise?"

He bristled at his twin challenging him. "I'd rather start off keeping it private and civil, not drag Stella through some kind of legal battle."

Shades of his mother and no less irritating, Claire patted his hand. "I understand. I meant you and Fiona could get together with a mediator."

He stabbed a broccoli stalk. "Are you suggesting Renee? I know she's a qualified counselor, but I'm not comfortable with our baby sister mediating my life."

She slapped the hand she'd been patting. "Not Renee. I was thinking Connor."

"Fiona might not agree. I haven't seen her at Sunday services." He would have remembered.

"That doesn't mean she wouldn't agree."

"I guess. She may prefer someone else, like her pastor, if she belongs to another church."

"You said Fiona wants to be part of the family, so play the family angle. Connor is Stella's uncle, but by marriage, so he's one level removed."

"You might have something there. I'll call the lawyer again and run that by her, see what she thinks about Christian mediation before anything legal. And speaking of family, keep this between the two of us for now. If and when anyone else needs to know, I'll tell them."

"Okay, mum's the word." Claire ran her thumb and forefinger across her lips.

Marc pushed away his food container. Supper had lost what little flavor it had had. He pulled out his cell phone. "It's not six yet. If you don't mind, I'm going to go into the other room and see if I can catch the lawyer before she leaves. I'll let you know later what I decide."

"That's fine. I'll be praying for you and Stella."

"I appreciate it," he said, powering up his phone to see Stella's baby face smiling at him from the screen. He didn't want to admit it, but he could see Fiona in her. He was going to need all the prayers he could get.

Chapter Three

Lost in her thoughts, Fiona almost missed the turn into the Hazardtown Community Church parking lot. Meeting with Pastor Connor seemed like a good idea. Marc had contacted her all businesslike on Monday with a couple items his partners wanted to include in the contract between the research farm and the restaurant partnership. Then he'd tackled the elephant in the room with an invitation to talk with him and Pastor Connor tonight about her *claim* that Stella was her niece.

Stepping from her car, she kicked a muddy chunk of snow out of her path. She knew in her heart that the little girl was her niece. And she had no intention of contesting Stella's adoption. After her failure with Mairi, she didn't want the responsibility of Stella, only to be part of her extended family.

Fiona walked into the church, the door closing behind her with a soft thud. The pastor's office was almost directly in front of her, as Marc had told her on the phone. Or she assumed it was the pastor's office. The door was open, but she didn't see anyone, only a desk with a computer and some bookshelves.

She stood in the doorway bumping her knee against

her briefcase. It was nearly six thirty, the time they'd set. She knew she was in the right place. Marc had given her the choice of meeting at the pastor's office here or at his home. When he'd mentioned that the pastor was his brother-in-law, she'd hesitated before deciding they'd be on more equal grounds at the church. Fiona smoothed the wrinkles from the skirt of her green linen dress.

Or maybe not. From what she'd seen, Marc and his family were active in the church. While Fiona considered herself a believer, she hadn't attended any church regularly since she'd worked in Guam, and then it was more because most of her neighbors and the people she worked with attended services than any real compulsion to be part of a church community.

"Here's the video of him and Natalie."

A male voice sounded from behind an almost closed door at the back of the room. A door that at first glance had appeared to lead to a closet. But it had a sign: Pastor's Office.

"I've got one of Stella on the rug in the church hallway this morning after preschool, showing me how she learned to do a somersault."

Marc. Fiona crossed the outer office toward the men's chuckles, hungry to see the video of Stella. She stopped herself from barging in and knocked on the door instead.

"Come in," Pastor Connor said.

She pushed the door open.

"Hi. Take a seat. Marc and I were kid-video warring."

He handed her his phone as she took the chair next to Marc, facing the desk.

"My son, Luc," he said, "dancing to my wife's piano playing."

The toddler in the video stole her voice for a minute. He was a miniature Marc. "Cute." She smiled and handed back the phone.

"Obviously, he takes after Natalie's side of the family, but that's certainly not a bad thing."

Another Delacroix sister. Fiona glanced sideways at Marc. *No, not a bad thing at all.*

"For you, it's a good thing." Marc razzed his brother-in-law. "You should be grateful."

Fiona repositioned herself in her chair, unsettled by the easy back-and-forth between the two men and uncertain that Marc and Connor's apparent closeness was a good thing for her, if Connor was going to mediate. "So, what did you have in the competition?" she asked, turning to Marc in an effort to join the friendly banter.

He tilted his head, looking confused. "Oh." He followed her gaze to his phone. "A video of Stella doing a somersault." He made no move to share it.

She swallowed away the painful tightness in her throat and focused her attention on Pastor Connor.

"Let's begin with prayer." He reached his hands across the desk to her and Marc.

Marc took her hand as if it were the perfectly natural thing to do. Maybe it was for them. They were family. She tightened her jaw and curved her fingers around Marc's hand. She was Stella's family, too.

"Dear Lord, be with us this evening and, with Your infinite wisdom, give Marc and Fiona and myself the guidance we need to do Your will. In Jesus's name, amen."

"Amen," she whispered, lifting her head when the men released her hands.

"I talked with the lawyer who handled Stella's adoption," Marc said, moving a folder from his left to front and center on the desk. "Copies of all of the documents are here."

"Wait." Pastor Connor laid his palm on top of the folder. "I have a good idea of what you want out of this meeting, Marc. I need to know what Fiona wants. Then we can get to details."

"First and foremost, stability." Fiona paused. "My mother moved us around a lot, looking for something better that she never found. She died when I was nineteen and Mairi was fifteen." She faltered, not used to talking about her family. "I'm only asking for a part in Stella's life as her aunt. I don't want to contest the adoption. I have no doubt it's valid or that Stella is where she's supposed to be."

Marc's chair creaked as he leaned forward. "You said you had proof Stella's your niece."

Connor frowned at the interruption.

"I do." Fiona lifted her case onto the desktop. "I've made copies of everything I have. But I think this is the proof you want." She lifted the papers from the case and placed them in front of Marc with a photo of Mairi at three and her at seven on top.

He sucked in a breath.

Fiona had felt the same sucker punch when she'd gotten out the battered family photo album Friday after her appointment with Autumn. There was no way anyone could deny the family resemblance.

She'd claimed the album as a child. It had come with her when, after her stepfather had left, her mother had dragged Fiona, Mairi and their baby sister, Elsbeth, all over northern Vermont and New Hampshire from each promised new start to the next. She'd brought it with her when she and Mairi had moved to Ithaca after their mother's fatal accident, so Fiona could attend college. And the album had made the trip to Guam and back.

She cleared her throat. "Certified copies of my, Mairi's and Stella's birth certificates and the Ticonderoga Birthing Center's record of Stella's birth," she said for Pastor Connor's benefit.

"Where did you get the birth certificate for Stella?" Marc asked. "My understanding is that her original one is in the sealed records at the adoption agency."

"I don't know about that. The certificate I have was in an envelope addressed to me with a letter my sister never sent." Fiona stopped so her voice wouldn't crack. "I had no idea until I received a package from the lawyer I hired to settle Mairi's estate. It came the day after we met at the farm."

The masculine planes of Marc's face softened. He tapped Stella's certificate with his finger. "Stella was only eight weeks old when she was placed with us. Your sister couldn't have kept her long."

"About a month, according to the information Autumn Hanlon gave me." Fiona bit her lip. She had no idea where her sister had been for that month. Mairi had checked into the cabin where she died only the evening before. "I think Mairi may have intended to give her baby up for adoption all along, just wanted a little time with her first."

"You think?"

"She didn't confide in me." Fiona's stomach tightened. Mairi had probably been afraid she'd be disappointed in her, as her letter seemed to say. Fiona had been so strident about neither one of them ending up like their mother. "I didn't know about Stella."

Marc's eyes narrowed. "Over nine months' time, I

think I would have noticed if any of my sisters were pregnant."

"Marc," Pastor Connor cautioned.

"During Mairi's pregnancy, I was in Guam managing the USDA farm there." She pinned Marc with a gaze. "You know that from my professional profile I gave you. Mairi and I talked and emailed, but after she drove me to the airport for my flight to Tamuning…" She closed her eyes. This time, she couldn't swallow the emotion that clogged her throat. "I never saw her alive again."

A warm male hand covered hers, and her eyes flew open to Pastor Connor pushing away from the desk. It was Marc's hand, giving her hope that despite his antagonism, they could work something out.

"I'll get you some water," Pastor Connor said. He left the office.

Marc's hand tightened on hers. "I'm sorry I was so rude. Are you okay?"

"I'm fine." Fiona allowed herself to take comfort from his strength and wonder what it would be like to have a man like Marc care for her.

He removed his hand from hers. "I can't imagine how I'd handle it if it had been one of my siblings. That's when you came back to the US?"

"I came back for a couple weeks when the authorities contacted me, and then finished my contract in Guam." She didn't need to tell him now that her sister had used a false name to rent the cabin, nor how long Mairi had lain in the morgue as a Jane Doe until she could be identified from her fingerprints on record for her nursing license, and while Fiona was located.

"Where do we go from here?" she asked.

"We get together again to work out details." He sounded as drained as she was.

"I'm willing to work with your lawyer, to put together something official."

"No, I was thinking along the lines of telling the rest of the family, introducing you to them and Stella. You haven't really met her, except the other day at the doctor's office. We're going to have to handle Stella's getting to know you carefully." He dropped his gaze to his hands on the desk. "Since Cate, my wife, died, Stella has verged on being hostile toward women with light-colored hair, who remind her of her mother."

Had Marc emphasized *mother*, or had that been her nerves triggering her imagination? On Friday, Stella had clung to Marc and hidden behind his leg, but she hadn't been hostile. Or was that Fiona's longing coloring her perception?

Pastor Connor placed a cup of water in front of her. "You two can work out meeting the family and whatever other details you think are necessary. But I have a recommendation to help Stella adjust."

Hope rose in Fiona.

Pastor Connor met her gaze, then Marc's. "It's what I'd do if she were mine."

Marc folded the last of the clothes from the dryer and walked into the living room to wake Stella from her nap. He and Stella *and* Fiona were all going to go to the introductory meeting of his sister Renee's new toddlers Bridges group tomorrow morning. As far as he could tell from his sister's enthusiastic description and the literature she'd given him, Bridges was a program for broken families.

He sighed. He guessed that's what he and Stella were,

and he was feeling it more since Fiona had dropped her bombshell.

Marc ran his fingers through his hair. He hadn't had any other choice but to agree to have Stella participate in the group, not after the way Fiona's face had lit up when Connor had couched his recommendation for Stella in such a personal way. And he'd given into Connor's other suggestion that he and Fiona try the Bridges groups for parents that Renee's supervisor at the Christian Action Coalition was starting. For Fiona. He'd been there, done that already with grief counseling.

Agreeing had given him some breathing room, time to investigate Fiona as much as he could. Before they'd left Connor's office, he and Fiona had agreed to put off getting together until after the Bridges meeting. Tonight he was taking his mom and dad out for a Friday fish fry to update them.

Looking down at his daughter's sleeping face, her long red-brown lashes resting on her plump baby cheeks, he hated to disturb her. Were Fiona's lashes red-brown, too? He couldn't recall.

"Stella, sweetpea." Marc touched her shoulder and she blinked her eyes open. Eyes that were the same golden hazel as Fiona's. "Time to wake and go to Aunt Natalie and Uncle Connor's house to play with Luc."

Stella sat up. "Luc? Luc at school. Stella go to school?"

He took her wanting to go back to preschool after spending the morning there as a positive sign. While Stella hadn't resisted going, she hadn't talked much about school, either, even when he'd prompted her. So he didn't know whether she liked playing with the other kids or how she'd react to going to Renee's group.

"No, not school. Aunt Natalie and Uncle Connor's to

play with Luc," Marc repeated. "Remember? I told you when I picked you up at school? Daddy has a meeting."

Stella nodded and climbed off the couch. "Burgers and ice cream."

He laughed. "Yes, you guys are going out for hamburgers. I didn't know about the ice cream."

His daughter nodded emphatically. "Ice cream. Stella's ready."

Looking at her bedhead mop of curls, Marc laughed with love and wonder that God had given him such a treasure, a treasure he wanted to feel secure enough about that he could share her with Fiona.

"Let me brush your hair first."

"'Rette?" Stella asked.

"Sure. I can put a barrette in it."

He got her ready and over to the parsonage with plenty of time to spare to drive to the restaurant in Schroon Lake where he was meeting his parents.

"Give Daddy kisses."

Stella bussed his cheek, and he rubbed noses with her before he placed her down in the parsonage kitchen.

"You be a good girl for Aunt Natalie." He shifted his weight from foot to foot. Stella had never stayed with Nat before, but she obviously liked her cousin Luc, and the restaurant where he was meeting his parents wasn't far from the parsonage or the Paradox Lake General Store, where Natalie and Connor were taking the kids.

"Stella good girl. Big girl." She stood tall as if trying to match the height of her slightly younger, but taller cousin.

"All right, then. I'll be back as soon as I can."

"Daddy come back."

Was that a quaver in her voice? No, she seemed okay.

"We'll be fine," Natalie said.

His sister probably knew better than him. He grimaced. Even as Stella's only parent for a good part of her life, with his long work hours in New York, he was sure he'd spent less physical time with Stella than Natalie had with Luc.

"Let us know how it goes," Connor added.

Marc gave him a noncommittal nod and left.

His parents' car was already parked in front of the restaurant when he drove up. The dashboard clock said he was ten minutes early, right on time for his scheduled plan to be there first, get a booth and have the upper hand from the start. But he hadn't accounted for Dad's philosophy that being on time was being fifteen minutes early. He pulled into a space a ways down the street and walked to the restaurant.

"Good evening," said a waitress who looked familiar, but he couldn't place. "Find a seat and I'll be right with you."

"Marc," his mother called from the booth where he'd already spotted them.

The waitress smiled and handed him a menu.

"Thanks," he said, finally recognizing her as someone who'd been a few years behind him in high school. Marc walked to the booth and slid into the seat across from his parents.

"So," his mother said, "what's the big news that merits you treating us to a meal you're not cooking? Did you get the revitalization grant for La Table Frais?"

"Terry," his dad cautioned. "Let the man catch a breath and look at the menu."

"All right. You know, you could have brought Stella." His mother glanced around the restaurant at the numerous families with children.

"I know, but I thought it would be nice to have an adult dinner with you."

His father tapped the menu on the table in front of him. "I'm going to have the fish fry special."

"Me, too," Marc said.

"Guys, did you even look at the other specials?" his mother asked.

"Why would I, when I came in knowing what I want?" his father answered.

Marc laughed. This was an ongoing dialogue between his parents that went back as far as he could remember.

The waitress came and took their orders, and they had their food in front of them in no time.

Marc pressed the side of his fork through the tip of his battered fried fillet. It was time for his announcement. The prospect took him back to high school, the day he told his parents he wanted to study culinary arts in college and not farm management, that he didn't want to be part of John Delacroix and Sons. Dad had mellowed a lot since then. But what he had to say tonight would hit Mom harder.

Marc cleared his throat. "I met a woman, a friend of Claire's, one of her coworkers."

"Oh." His mother's eyes brightened.

Bad start. "A business meeting. Fiona Bryce. She's the new farm-to-table liaison."

His father nodded. "I read about that program and her hiring in the *Times of Ti*. She's a Cornell grad, like Claire."

"Yes, a couple years behind Claire," Marc said. One of the things he'd found in his online search about Fiona. "Claire suggested Fiona and I talk about how she can work with me, setting up connections with local food producers."

"Do it," his father encouraged. "The Cornell people know what they're doing."

His father's words frustrated him. It wasn't that Dad wasn't proud of him graduating from the Culinary Institute or his youngest sister from the University at Albany, but he was inordinately proud of Claire and Marc's younger brother, Paul, being Cornell graduates. His father had wanted to go to Cornell, but for financial and family reasons had settled for a two-year degree in dairy production and management from a state college.

"I already have a contract." Fiona had wasted no time emailing it to him. "My partners are reviewing it. But there's something else I want to tell you about Fiona."

Both of his parents stopped eating and looked at him, his mother's brow creased with concern.

Had it been something in his voice? "It's nothing bad." *At least I hope it's not.* "I mean, it's good. I wanted to tell you first because it affects the whole family."

His mother made a show of wiping her hands on her napkin and placing it back on her lap. "You're interested in this woman enough to want to tell us? You just met her."

"No, not in the way you're thinking." Although his thoughts had gone in that direction, too—until Fiona's claim to Stella had turned his world upside down. Marc gripped the table edge as if that would give him the extra boost of strength he needed. "Fiona is Stella's biological aunt."

The tension in his muscles went into overtime while he waited for their reaction.

"Is that what she told you?" his mother asked.

"Told and showed me. Stella's birth mother, Fiona's

sister, is dead. Fiona had a copy of Stella's original birth certificate and the Ticonderoga Birthing Center's record of Stella's birth, among other things. I talked with Autumn. She delivered Stella, and the birthing center released her to Precious in His Sight when Fiona's sister returned with her a few weeks later to give her up for adoption."

"You can't let this woman take Stella from us."

Red spots flashed in front of his eyes. "Fiona says she simply wants to be an aunt to Stella."

"And you believe her? What do you know about the woman?"

"Terry." His father placed his hand over his mother's, the note of warning in his voice loud and clear.

Well, to Marc, at least. He wasn't so sure about his mother.

"It was a sealed adoption," Marc said. "I talked with the lawyer who handled it. Fiona has no legal grounds to contest it."

"I see," his father said.

"But what do you know about her?" his mother repeated.

Marc bit his tongue. Should he have prepared a dossier? "She's Claire's friend, and I haven't found anything in my searching that shows she's anything other than what she says. And now we can know more about Stella's medical history if we ever need to, and answer her questions when she's older and starts asking." He faced his father. "You know I'd protect Stella with my life."

His father nodded, understanding showing in his eyes.

"You can't mean to just bring her into your...our family," his mother said.

Marc sensed a tone of almost fear in her voice. Mom was always so open and giving. When he was growing up, their house had been a haven to any of their friends needing one.

"Stella isn't ready to be told who Fiona is," he said. "We'll be working on that in the Bridges program."

"This Fiona is going to be part of that?" his mother asked.

"Yes, we talked with Connor about it Wednesday evening."

"You've known since Wednesday?" His mother pressed her lips together.

He wasn't about to admit that he'd known in his gut for a week, since Fiona had told him on the phone. "All three of us are going to the Bridges meeting tomorrow, and I plan to invite Fiona to Sunday dinner at the house."

He hadn't actually planned to, not until this minute. But something inside him wanted to crack his mother's uncharacteristically stony facade, to open her up to the family accepting Fiona.

Because, he realized suddenly, he wanted to accept her.

Chapter Four

Fiona breathed in a deep lungful of the crisp mountain air before she pulled open the door to the Hazardtown Community Church hall. She'd gone back and forth as to whether it would be better to be one of the first to arrive for the Bridges meeting or one of the last, and had decided on last. She hadn't wanted to risk being there with only Marc, Stella and the meeting leader, even though that was the idea of the Bridges program, to help bring together members of changing families.

Fiona swallowed, remembering what Marc had said about Stella's hostility toward women like her. Perhaps arriving early when fewer people were here may have been better after all, given that she didn't know how Stella would react to her.

Too late now. She stepped into the hall, the door closing behind her with a startling bang that brought everyone's attention to her.

"Welcome," a man called to her.

"Hi." Fiona looked past him to the table where the group was gathered, searching for Stella. She saw only adults, and her gaze settled on Marc's expressionless face. The others blurred around him. She set her jaw against the shudder that threatened her composure. She wasn't that poor little Bryce girl anymore that everyone had been quick to pity, no matter how little time her family spent in one place.

"I'm Noah Phelps, the group facilitator," said the man who'd greeted her. "You must be Fiona."

Fiona pulled her focus from Marc. She lifted her chin. She'd been the last to arrive. Not the unobtrusive entry she might have wanted, but she'd accomplished her goal of not being alone with Marc and Stella.

"Come join us," Noah said. "We were about to go around the table and introduce ourselves."

Fiona slipped into an empty chair kitty-corner across the table from Marc.

"As you already know, I'm the director of the Bridges program at the Christian Action Coalition. I'll be moderating the group. Unlike the children's programs Bridges offers, this group will focus on the needs of the adults in the transitioning families. Let me remind you of the confidentiality agreement you all signed when you registered for the group. What we share in group stays in group."

Absorbing Noah's words, Fiona looked around the table. Most of the people appeared to be couples, except for one, an older woman with a twentysomething man that might be a mother–son or mother-in-law and son-in-law pair.

Noah continued, "This group is as much or more about your sharing what you've found works for your family as it is about my providing guidance to give your new family structure a solid start."

Fiona gazed down at her hands, running one thumbnail against a rough edge of another. She wasn't against getting some guidance to use as a ruler against her perceptions. The promising start she'd made with Marc businesswise—his asking for a contract before his partners had agreed—hadn't carried over when their situation became personal. And the start she'd thought she'd provided Mairi had crumbled when Fiona hadn't been there to hold it up.

She shouldn't be surprised. That had been her life. The glimmer of something going well followed by crushing reality. Her stepfather's new job that had ended up being a prelude to his leaving. Her mother's multiple promises of a new start. Fiona's optimism when a teacher at her first high school had taken an interest in her, only to have her mother pull her out of the school a few months later for another new start. Fiona pulled her hands apart and straightened. That's why she meant to be there for Stella, to carry through—no matter what it took.

"I've done enough talking. Now it's your turn." Noah motioned to the person on his right. The people between Noah and Marc shared about themselves and their families.

Fiona had been wrong. A few of those attending were single, divorced or widowed, with children. Had Marc signed on for the group before she'd told him Stella was her sister's child? For whatever reason, that thought relaxed her.

"I'm Marc Delacroix."

Fiona focused on Marc.

"I have a daughter, Stella, who's almost three."

Fiona's stomach flip-flopped at the emotion in Marc's voice when he said Stella's name.

"My wife, Cate, died of cancer almost two years ago, and after a tough time of it on our own, I moved here with Stella to be close to my family." He glanced at

Fiona for a split second before looking away and taking a deep breath. "Stella is adopted, and this week I learned that she has an aunt in the area on her birth mother's side. So Stella is adjusting to new family on both sides."

The introductions moved around the table to Fiona. She'd been right that the older woman and younger man were an in-law combination, and one of the other women was an aunt raising a niece whose parents had abandoned her.

"Fiona," Noah prompted her.

"Hi, I'm Fiona Bryce, and I'm the aunt Marc mentioned."

She glanced across the table and ignored the frown Marc shot her for sharing the detail he hadn't. Why wouldn't she tell the group? They needed to know why she was here. She hadn't brought a child with her. Besides, this was a small town. The information would be out soon anyway, even if no one here leaked it. That's the way it was.

"I was working out of the country. I returned briefly after I was notified of my sister's death, but I didn't know I had a niece until last week." She lowered her gaze to the table to avoid any looks of sympathy in the other people's eyes so she could get through her introduction. "Stella doesn't know who I am—yet." Fiona smiled around the table, ending with Marc. "That's it."

"Thanks, Fiona, everyone," Noah said. "I'll let Renee know she can bring the children back in."

The woman next to Fiona nudged her elbow. "Noah had his coworker take the kids to one of the Sunday school rooms to play while we had our meeting."

"I wondered where they were. The pastor said we'd be interacting with the kids." She bit her lip. *Interacting.* That sounded stilted and impersonal.

"Fiona," the woman sitting next to Marc said—the other aunt in the group. "Do you want to trade places since you're with Marc?"

She wasn't exactly with him. Fiona looked to Marc for direction, considering Stella would be returning to him when the kids came back. He'd assumed the reserved expression he'd had when she'd joined the group at the table, which irritated her. They were supposed to be working together for Stella.

"Yes," she said, louder than she'd intended. "Thanks."

She and the woman changed places, with Fiona positioning her chair as far from Marc as she could without looking like that was her intention, which it wasn't entirely. She wanted space for Stella to climb on his lap, as well as a buffer between her and the guarded signals radiating from the stoic-looking man beside her.

The sound of high-pitched voices and little feet preceded the children's appearance at the inner door to the hall. Noah led the children in, with a woman who looked so much like Claire and Marc that she had to be another sister or other relative following behind, holding Stella's hand.

"My youngest sister, Renee." Marc answered the question in her mind with a chin lift toward the door.

Fiona felt Renee's gaze on her before she saw it. "She knows?"

"Yes. She works with Noah, and I told my parents the other night," Marc said.

His face didn't give her a clue as to how they'd reacted. She counted the family members who knew: Marc's parents, his brother-in-law Pastor Connor and, Fiona assumed, Marc's other sister Natalie, the pastor's wife.

Renee walked the children to their parents and

guardians, bringing Stella over to Marc last and approaching him from the side opposite Fiona. The little girl scrambled onto Marc's lap and gave him a big hug. A wave of longing for her sister, for family, rolled over Fiona.

"No Luc today," Stella said.

"Luc's our sister Natalie's little boy," Marc said.

Fiona remembered. The toddler in the video Pastor Connor had showed her.

"He goes to preschool with Stella." Renee had walked around behind Marc's chair. "I'm Renee Maddox, Marc's sister."

"Fiona Bryce." She met Renee's blatant perusal and reached around her obvious baby bump to shake her hand.

Fiona dropped her hand to her lap as Renee left to join Noah at the head of the table. She was going to have to get Marc aside and talk with him about her meeting his family, preferably one or two at a time. That way, she could talk with each of them personally before they set themselves against her as a group.

Marc's low voice answering Stella's chatter brought back her longing. He had a whole army of people behind him. Her throat clogged. She only had herself to rely on to make a family with Stella.

"So you had a good time with the kids and Aunt Renee?" Marc asked.

Stella nodded at him. "Aunt Nay."

That made three of his sisters that Stella had been willing to go along with, without him, although she hadn't said more than a word or two to any of them. He glanced over his shoulder at Fiona, whose eyes were fixed on Stella with a look that he could only describe as hunger. He tightened his grip on his daughter.

She pushed away. "No hugs, Daddy. Balloons."

He followed her pointer finger to Noah and Renee, who were pulling balloons from an industrial-size trash bag.

"We're going to have balloon races, with cookies and juice afterward and balloons for everyone to take home," Noah announced.

Marc turned to Fiona. "Before you got here, Noah explained that the game will give him and Renee an opportunity to study the family dynamics, as Noah said."

Fiona stiffened before she answered. "I see."

Marc sympathized. He couldn't say that he felt any more comfortable than Fiona seemed to.

Noah motioned to them. "Everyone up here with their family partner. Kat and Lydia, Renee and I will be your partners," he said to the woman who had changed places with Fiona, and another woman who was here by herself. "The object of the game is to pass a balloon back and forth with your child until you get to your partner on the other side of the room. Then your partner will pass it back and forth until he or she and your child are back here."

Marc stood, placed Stella on the floor and took her hand. "Let's go." He smiled and motioned to include Fiona. She returned a half smile and followed slightly behind.

"One of you and your child line up here." Noah directed them to a line of blue tape on the floor. "The other needs to be across the room with Renee for the second leg of the race."

"I'll go first," Marc said.

Fiona nodded and started across the room.

"No." Stella stamped her foot as if she'd just noticed Fiona. "Not her. Aunt Nay."

Fiona stopped, frozen in her tracks, waiting.

"Go ahead, Fiona," Noah said before Marc could re-assure his daughter.

He turned a steely gaze on the director, not waiting to see what Fiona was doing. Renee had said she'd told Noah about Stella's aversion to lighter-haired women and the meltdown she'd had when the woman in the grocery store had talked to her, and Fiona had just said Stella didn't know her yet. Was the man trying to set off his baby so he could observe them?

"I could switch places with Renee." Fiona was back beside him.

"Aunt Nay," Stella repeated in a relatively calm voice.

Noah raised his hand like a stop sign before squat-ting to Stella's level.

Marc sucked in a breath and sensed Fiona close be-side him doing the same. He checked the impulse to tell Noah to back off his little girl. But he'd only give him so much leeway.

"Stella, your aunt Renee has to do her job with her team on the other side of the room. Do you know what a job is?"

She nodded. "Stella puts socks away for Daddy."

Marc released his breath in a whoosh when she an-swered Noah. He and Stella played catch with rolled socks from the laundry basket, with her tossing them in the open drawer.

"That's an important job," Noah said. "Your aunt Renee has a job, too. She needs to help her team get its balloon back to this side of the room. Fiona is on your team. It's her job to help you get your balloon back."

"No Feena," Stella said.

"Do you know Fiona?" Noah asked, waving her over.

What was Noah doing now? He tapped his toe on the blue tape. They could simply sit out and let the others play.

"Stella, this is Fiona. Fiona, this is Stella," Noah introduced them.

"Hi, Stella," Fiona said.

Marc clenched his fists to his side, waiting.

"I'm your…"

She wouldn't. He hadn't liked it, but he understood why Fiona had told the group. But telling Stella that Fiona was family here, in front of a room of strangers… His clench tightened. Mom was right. What did he know about Fiona Bryce?

"I'm your daddy's friend, and I'd like to be yours."

The tension drained from him, replaced by admiration for Fiona's sensitivity. "Yes, Fiona is Daddy's friend."

Sunday dinner couldn't come fast enough. The sooner his family all knew, the better. And he liked the idea of Fiona being presented to others as a friend, for now. She *was* Claire's friend. Marc ran his gaze over Fiona's delicate features, and the attraction that had surprised him when they'd first met returned. Maybe he liked the idea too much.

Stella turned her back to Fiona and wrapped her arms around Marc's leg. "Stella no talk Feena," she said into the denim of his jeans.

Marc placed his hand on Stella's coppery curls and glanced from Fiona to Noah. Both were nodding.

"No, you don't have to talk with Fiona," he said, relieved that they understood. Today was the most Stella had interacted with anyone but him in almost longer than he could remember.

Stella pulled away and tipped her face up to Noah. "Stella do balloons."

When he turned to celebrate the moment with Fiona, she was already almost across the room. His shoulders slumped. What was with him? He set his jaw. It wasn't as if they really were friends.

The balloon races had everyone laughing—the little ones with the joy of throwing, punching, kicking or otherwise getting their team balloons to their partners and running ahead to receive the partner's pass, and the adults at the children's efforts.

His team's balloon crossed the blue-tape finish line with what looked like an unplanned dropkick by Stella, followed by her and Fiona trotting across the line.

Marc scooped up Stella and spun her around. "That's my girl."

She giggled, a sound he heard far too infrequently.

He placed her down and rose, arms still open, to face Fiona. By impulse, he leaned forward as she stepped toward him. Time halted for a second when he caught Fiona's eyes widen and readjusted his movement from a congratulatory hug to a pat on the back.

"Nice job, partner."

A little hand patted his leg. "Nice job, Daddy."

Fiona laughed, defusing whatever subconscious thought had drawn him to her. It was probably that he just plain missed being a complete family.

"That was some competition," Noah said. "I see our helper, Mrs. Donnelly, has the cookies and juice all ready."

Marc had been so into the race and watching Stella and Fiona that he hadn't even noticed Natalie there. She must have entered the hall through the kitchen door.

Noah motioned to a long table set up on the kitchen

side of the hall. "Everyone take a seat. There are plenty of chairs."

Marc took his daughter's hand and looked at Fiona. "Come on, team. Let's find our seats."

He sat with Stella on one side and Fiona on the other, and after the simple grace of *God is great, God is good, so we thank Him for this food*, Natalie walked over to the empty seat on the other side of Fiona.

"Is this seat taken?" she asked.

Marc tensed. What was his sister up to?

"No," Fiona said.

Her response was neutral, but she appeared to sit up straighter. Or maybe he'd only imagined it.

Natalie pulled out the chair and sat. "I see Noah paired you up with my brother and Stella. We haven't met." But his sister probably knew who Fiona was. He hadn't told Connor not to tell her. "I'm Marc's sister Natalie Donnelly," she continued.

"Fiona Bryce. Nice to meet you," Fiona said.

"Fiona?" Natalie said, her voice rising.

Marc's air passages constricted. *Here it comes. Connor must have told Natalie.* He looked sideways at his sister to see if her face registered any of the hostility Mom had expressed. Natalie looked more as if she were trying to place Fiona's name.

"You work with Claire at the farm. She's mentioned you."

"Yes."

Natalie said something in reply that Marc didn't hear. He was too busy rolling his shoulders in relief from the weight that had lifted from them. He'd made the right decision to ask Fiona to the family's Sunday dinner. No way were his nerves up to him not knowing who knew about her and who didn't know or making individual introductions repeatedly. Sunday dinner couldn't come fast enough, assuming Fiona agreed to go.

A teenaged girl with long dark hair answered Fiona's knock on the front door of the rambling white farmhouse.

"Hi, you must be Uncle Marc's girlfriend, Fiona. I'm Aimee."

Fiona stumbled on the small step into the house. Is that what the Delacroixs thought? That Marc had invited her to dinner because they were dating? She'd tried to decline the family dinner invitation and explained how she thought getting together with family members individually would be better. But he'd been adamant.

"I'm Fiona Bryce. I work with your aunt Claire, and I'm not your uncle's girlfriend." Had her words sounded as strident to the girl as they had to her?

Aimee shrugged. "Uncle Marc! Fiona's here!" she shouted from the front hall into the adjacent room.

Fiona followed Aimee into the living room where Marc, Stella, Luc and another dark-haired boy were gathered around the coffee table playing Candyland. With all the electronic games available these days, Fiona didn't know kids still played board games. An older man, who had to be Marc's father, sat in a recliner watching.

Marc rose from the couch. "Fiona, hi. Join us." He motioned to the seat beside where he'd been sitting. "This is my dad."

"Nice to meet you, Mr. Delacroix."

"Call me John." He glanced at Stella and back to Fiona.

Her welcoming smile froze. Was he sizing her up?

"I've read all about your program at the Willsboro farm. Let's talk later with my other son, Paul. We're partners. Most of our milk is going into yogurt, but we might want to get in on your program, too."

"Sounds good." Fiona walked by John, around the coffee table where the game was set up and perched on the edge of the couch.

Marc sat. "You met Aimee." The teen had already left the room. "She's my oldest niece. Her sister, Amelia, is a few minutes younger."

"More twins."

"Yep," he said, "the only ones in that generation so far." He pointed at the older boy kneeling across the table. "This guy is their younger brother. Robbie, Fiona is my and Aunt Claire's friend."

"Hi, Robbie."

"Hi. Do you want to play the next game?"

"No," Stella said.

Fiona made the eye contact she'd been avoiding since she'd entered the room. She stiffened at the defiance on the little girl's face.

"Stella, that wasn't nice," Marc said. "Tell Fiona you're sorry."

The little girl stuck out her lower lip.

"That's okay," Fiona said, not wanting to make the relationship any worse.

"No, it's not. Stella, tell Fiona you're sorry or go to time-out."

"Sorry," she spat.

"That's Luc next to Robbie," Marc continued.

"Ah, the star of Pastor Connor's video."

"The one with Luc dancing?" Marc's father asked. "That was a hoot, wasn't it?"

"It was."

"Did you see the one with Stella somersaulting?"

"No, I didn't." Although at the meeting with Pastor Connor, she remembered wanting to.

Marc leaned forward. "It's your turn, Stella. Pick a card and I'll help you move."

"Red." She waved the card.

"Right. Where's the next red space?" Marc asked.

"Here." Stella pointed with a big grin that pierced Fiona's heart. What she wouldn't give for that smile to be for her. In time, she hoped.

"Hey, Stella's hair is the same color as yours," Robbie said.

Stella dropped her card and covered her hair with her hands, as if to protect it from being snatched from her head. "My hair."

Marc and his father exchanged a look, and the corners of Marc's lips curved up at Stella's comical gesture before he opened his mouth to speak.

"Okay, everybody," Claire interrupted from the doorway to the dining room. "Paul's in from the barn. We can eat. Hey, Fiona, glad you could come."

Fiona rose, wondering how glad Claire would be after Marc shared their news.

Marc and his dad walked her to the dining room, while Claire herded the three kids. Most of the rest of the family was already seated. Fiona hung back while Marc and Claire set up the kids at a small table.

His nephew beamed when Marc said, "You're in charge here, Robbie," before stepping to the family table and pulling out an empty chair for Fiona and one next to it for Claire.

She was a little surprised that Marc seemed as good with his nephews as he was with Stella. Her frame of reference for men was that they tolerated their own children—period.

"You're a good influence, Fiona," Claire said. "I can't remember when, if ever, Marc has pulled a chair out for me."

Fiona slipped into her seat, stomach churning. If only all of them could agree with Claire and still feel that way after dinner.

Marc sat on her other side. "I think you know everyone but my sister Andie, Robbie and the twins' mother, her husband, Rob, and Renee's husband, Rhys."

They welcomed her so warmly that for a moment Fiona let down the guard she'd perfected as a child and allowed herself to think maybe, just maybe, she could be a part of this family.

"What's keeping Mom?" Marc asked.

As if in answer, a woman who looked like an older version of Marc's sister Andie walked in carrying a huge bowl of mashed potatoes. "The potatoes got done early. I had to warm them up in the microwave." She placed the bowl on the table and sat next to her husband.

"You must be Fiona," Marc's mother stated, her voice lacking the warmth of the others' greetings.

"Nice to meet you, Mrs. Delacroix," Fiona said. Marc's mother's silence—no invitation to call her by her first name—struck Fiona as a thrown gauntlet. And the puzzled looks on most of her children's faces intensified the hurt Fiona should've been able to throw off, but couldn't.

Marc shifted in his seat, bumping her knee with his. "If you don't mind, Dad, I'd like to say grace."

"Go for it."

Claire and Marc reached for her hands. He wrapped

his hand around hers, and a warm rush of strength flowed through her when he gave it a squeeze.

Fiona bowed her head and cleared her mind.

"Dear Lord," Marc said, "thank you for this bountiful spread of food before us and for allowing us to be together to enjoy it. Open our hearts and minds to Your will and Your service. In Jesus's name, amen."

Please let this go well, Fiona entreated in her mind before whispering, "Amen."

Everyone started passing dishes around and jumping in and out of several different conversations going on.

Marc handed her a dish of green beans. "It can be overwhelming. That's one of the reasons I bought the little table for the kids. The first couple meals, I couldn't get Stella off my lap."

Fiona spooned out some beans and passed the dish on to Claire.

"I'll admit that family dinners of…" Fiona did a quick look around the table for a head count that ended on Marc's mother, giving her a seemingly disapproving stare.

"Sixteen," Claire filled in.

Fiona broke eye contact. "Of sixteen aren't what I'm used to." She couldn't say she'd even been to a family dinner half that large before, even when her grandparents had been alive.

For the rest of the meal, Fiona fielded a few questions about her job and where she was from. She'd answered, "Ticonderoga, originally," without providing further details. But she mostly picked at her food and listened to everyone talking and laughing around her. She'd never been good at small talk. Her mother had taught her to be closemouthed about their family life, and she'd had trouble shaking that as an adult.

When they'd finished eating, Marc's dad pushed his chair back a couple inches and patted his flat stomach. "You outdid yourself today, Terry."

Claire nudged her and whispered in Fiona's ear, "He says that every Sunday."

But Fiona's attention was on Marc's mother, who was smiling for the first smile Fiona had seen. This was more how she'd pictured Mrs. Delacroix.

"I'll help you get dessert and coffee, Mom." Claire stood and gave Marc a look that appeared to be some kind of secret communication.

Once Claire and his mother were in the kitchen, he cleared his throat. "I have something to tell you all."

Fiona gripped the napkin on her lap. Claire knew and hadn't said anything. But why would she? They were only casual work friends, and maybe Marc had asked her not to.

"Aimee and Amelia, please take your brother and Stella and Luc into the TV room and put a DVR on for them."

"Uncle Marc," the teens said in unison.

"We're not little kids like them," Amelia said.

"Your mother can tell you later, if she wants."

"You heard your uncle," their father said.

"Go ahead, son," Marc's father said when the kids were out of earshot.

"Fiona—Fiona and I—that is, we—" He seemed to catch his breath on the word *we*. "Fiona is Stella's birth mother's sister."

From their faces, Fiona could tell immediately who had already known and who hadn't. She took solace in the fact that she didn't face any stronger emotion than surprise.

"Stella doesn't know yet," Marc said. "Fiona and I

are working with Renee and Noah and will tell her when we all feel she's ready and can understand."

Her heart pulsed in her chest at Marc's emphasis on her inclusion in the decision.

"And none of this leaves this room until we know what's true," Marc's mother interjected as she placed a silver coffeepot on the table in front of Fiona with a thump.

"Mom." Marc pushed his chair back.

"Terry," his dad cautioned.

Fiona drew back inside herself to the old place where she was *that Bryce girl*, never fully accepted, always a little suspect. Marc touched her arm, and she returned to the present.

"I should have DNA results this week," she said. "Autumn Hanlon did the testing. Now, if you'll excuse me, I'd better go and let you discuss things in private."

"You don't have to," Marc said, his gaze fixed on his mother.

"Stay," Claire said.

Fiona didn't know if Claire was supporting her or Marc, but she'd take it. She rose. "Thank you for the delicious meal." For all her faults, her mother had done her best to teach her and her sisters manners as she knew them, and kindness. Kindness that wasn't often returned.

"I'll walk you out," Marc said.

"No. No, thank you." She didn't need any help escaping situations where she wasn't wanted. She had years of practice.

Chapter Five

Three days later, Marc paced the kitchen area of La Table Frais, checking the progress the contractor had made on enlarging the area and visualizing the placement of the new appliances he'd ordered. Except his mind kept replaying Sunday dinner rather than seeing the state-of-the-art stainless steel appliances installed. Despite prayers for understanding, he couldn't completely rid himself of his anger at Mom or his confusion about her attitude toward Fiona. Mom had always been open to all of their friends, making their home a haven to any of them who might have needed one.

From the bits of Fiona's life he'd picked up on, from conversations with her, their meeting with Connor and the online search he'd done, it sounded to him like Fiona could use a haven. He couldn't be that haven, as much as the thought tempted him at times. But he'd seen a yearning in Fiona when she was around Stella that both scared him and drew him to her. He'd hoped, still hoped, his family as a whole could assuage the yearning so it wasn't all focused on his daughter.

Marc pulled out his phone. How'd it go? he texted

Natalie, feeling like he was back in high school trying to pull something over on Mom.

Yesterday, while Mom was at the Adirondack Medical Center with the church visitation committee visiting a couple of members there, he'd had Dad watch Stella while he'd gone to pick out and arrange for the delivery of the appliances. Today, rather than asking Mom, he'd arranged for Natalie to pick up Stella from The Kids Place for a playdate with Luc so he could meet with Fiona and Autumn at the birthing center to go over the DNA testing. The testing had been Fiona's idea, but it could help with Mom's resistance.

Having to deal with family dynamics was one of the reasons he'd stayed away from Paradox Lake so long.

His phone pinged.

Fine, but she kind of picked at her lunch. Of course, my only comparison is chowhound Luc.

OK. I'll text when I leave the center.

He clasped his hands behind his neck and stretched. Stella hadn't said anything about her tummy this morning but had only eaten half of her cereal. It could have been because she liked school and was so excited about going to Luc's that she wasn't hungry—or because she didn't want to complain about not feeling well because he might keep her home.

He dropped his arms.

"How's it look, boss?" The work foreman and his crew had returned from lunch.

"Great. I've got the appliances coming next Thursday. Are you still on schedule for that?"

"No problem."

"All right. I'll let you guys get back to work." Marc took his time walking through the yet-to-be remodeled dining area and out to his SUV, then drove toward Ticonderoga.

As he closed in on the birthing center, he first lifted one hand from the grip he held on the steering wheel and flexed it, and then the other. Marc could see the scenario if the DNA testing showed Fiona was Stella's birth aunt. What might happen if the testing was negative was another story, except that it would make Mom happy. Would Fiona fade from his life, except for consulting on the restaurant opening? His hands tightened on the wheel again. But that's what he wanted, a business relationship. The friendly gestures at the Bridges meeting and Sunday dinner were for Stella's sake, not his.

He pulled into the center parking lot and looked for Fiona's car before he realized he didn't know what kind she drove. He didn't know much of anything about Fiona herself, beyond what he'd found online—old news stories about her mother's fatal accident and her sister's death, information about her academic and professional life—and the bits and pieces she'd reluctantly shared. Not that it excused Mom's uncharacteristic rudeness on Sunday, but she may have been on point when she questioned him on what he knew about Fiona.

He parked and stared at the building before throwing open the vehicle door, stepping out and slamming it behind him. Well, at least he'd learn something today.

Nostalgia flooded Marc as he walked to the check-in window. He and Cate hadn't used this center for their infertility testing, but the one they'd used hadn't looked substantially different. Check-in window, waiting room filled predominately with women and a health video playing on a television. Here, a corner with bright stencils on the wall delineated a children's area with books, toys and puzzles. At the bigger center he and Cate had used downstate, there had been a separate children's room off the waiting room.

"Hi," said the clerk at the window.

"Hi. Marc Delacroix to see Autumn. I…we have a 1:30 appointment."

The clerk looked behind him.

"I'm meeting the other person here."

"Have you been here before?" the clerk asked, reaching for a clipboard.

"No, but the person I'm meeting has."

"Okay, take a seat, and a nurse will call you."

Marc escaped through the archway into the waiting room and looked for Fiona, but she wasn't there yet.

"Hi, Marc," said Tessa Donnelly, his friend Josh's wife.

"Tessa. How's business at the Majestic?" He struck first to direct their conversation to business rather than why he was here.

"Not bad. But I have to say, I'm glad you chose Lake George for your restaurant, so you're not competing for my dinner theater patrons."

"Hey, isn't that what friends are for, looking out for each other?" The lightness of his reply faded. Was that why his mother's behavior disturbed him so much? He'd expected her, of all his family members, to have his back about Fiona for no other reason than he wanted her to. Was that why he'd felt so protective of Fiona at dinner? Because Mom wasn't? Marc pinched the bridge of his nose. Mom probably thought she was protecting him by being skeptical of Fiona. Couldn't she see he didn't need that kind of support, but that Fiona did?

"So how's the restaurant coming?"

"Good. I was down there this morning checking out the renovation progress. The kitchen equipment is arriving next week."

"Marc."

He and Tessa looked toward the doorway. "Hi, Fiona, have you met Tessa Donnelly?" he asked.

"Yes, hi, Tessa. I rent my apartment from her grandmother."

Marc filed away that piece of information. "We might as well take a seat." He scuffed the toe of his shoe on the flat gray rug as Tessa looked back and forth from him to Fiona.

"Good to see you both," Tessa said.

"Marc? Marc Delacroix, is that you?" a voice said from behind him and Fiona before they'd taken two steps toward the empty seats down the row from Tessa.

He stopped, recognizing Charlotte Russell's voice. She was someone he'd gone to high school with. What was this, homecoming week? Charlotte had also been one of the biggest gossips in Paradox Lake, although Claire had said Charlotte had reformed.

He turned. "Hey, Charlotte."

"Fiona Bryce," said a nurse who stepped into the waiting area.

Lifting his hand and giving his former schoolmate what he hoped was an apologetic smile, Marc said, "Gotta go. Nice seeing you." He trailed after Fiona and the nurse.

Marc hadn't considered that he might run into people he knew at the birthing center, or what they would think seeing him going in for an appointment with Fiona.

The nurse led them to Autumn's office. "Autumn will be with you in a few minutes."

They each took one of the seats facing Autumn's desk.

"That bad, huh?" Fiona said.

"What?"

"Your expression when we were walking from the waiting room."

He stretched his legs out under the desk. "I hadn't expected to run into people I know."

"I'm sure Tessa won't say anything."

"Right, but I can't say the same about Charlotte."

Fiona shrugged. "I don't know about you, but it wouldn't be the first time someone has judged me without knowing the facts." An undercurrent of bravado laced the nonchalant tone of her words.

Without thinking, he leaned toward Fiona and the undercurrent changed course, crashing over him in a wave of protectiveness toward her. He wanted to shield her against gossip, his mother and whatever Autumn might tell them.

As if in response, Fiona tilted her head and looked him directly in the eyes. His gaze fastened on her parted lips. Marc jerked back. *Get a grip.* This was about Stella. Not about Fiona.

And certainly not about him and Fiona.

Fiona tried to get comfortable in the chair. Her nerves had already been on high alert before Marc had leaned toward her, his eyes searching her face. Then, when he'd jerked away and shuttered whatever emotion he'd been feeling, it was as if he'd poured rubbing alcohol on her already inflamed synapses.

"Hi, guys." Autumn stepped into the office and closed the door behind her.

"Hi," Fiona squeaked, her heart welcoming Autumn's buffering presence while the dread in the pit of her stomach made her wish for more time to prepare for the test results.

Marc simply nodded.

Autumn placed a folder on the desk and took her seat behind it. "Marc, as I told Fiona, the testing is generally more definitive with a paternal aunt, but it can establish maternal lines, as well."

Fiona's dread blossomed into full-blown fear and discouragement. Was Autumn leading up to telling them the testing was inconclusive? If it was, she'd have to prove herself some other way. She slumped in her seat. She was so tired of proving herself over and over again. For a moment, Fiona had a glimpse of the despondency Mairi may have felt. Had she been part of fostering that?

Warmth enveloped her right hand, driving off some of the chill paralyzing her hope. Marc had placed his hand over hers on the chair arm.

"Are you all right?" he asked.

"As okay as I can be under the circumstances." She couldn't help the resentment that flared. No matter what the results, Marc still had Stella and the rest of his family.

"Then let me put you out of your misery." Autumn flipped open the folder and turned it around so the charts were readable to Fiona and Marc.

Fiona stared at the graphs of green and blue bars until they blurred into turquoise blobs.

"So what does it mean?" Marc asked, voicing the question her mind was shouting.

All of the air was sucked from the room. Fiona gnawed her thumbnail, a habit she'd broken years ago.

"What it means…" Autumn tapped one of the bars with her finger and it came back into focus for Fiona. "Is that there's a greater than eighty-seven percent chance that Fiona is Stella's aunt."

Fiona's eyes brimmed with tears as Autumn explained the significance of the various graphed results. It didn't matter that she was only hearing half of Autumn's words. Stella was her niece. A part of her sister lived on. God was giving her the opportunity to make it up to Mairi for not being here when she needed her.

"Eighty-seven percent."

Fiona caught the last part of Marc's sentence. After seeming to accept her as Stella's aunt before the test results, he was questioning it now?

"Pardon?" she asked, surprised that her voice sounded so normal.

"I was following Autumn's explanation of the results," Marc said.

"Oh." A huge weight lifted from her. But she had to ask, "You accept that I'm Stella's aunt?"

His hand squeezed hers. "I accepted that when I saw the picture of you and your sister."

Fiona felt Autumn's gaze on them and didn't want to interpret the soft smile the woman had on her face when Fiona looked at her. It was probably on par with what Fiona was feeling toward Marc right now—that she should *not* be feeling.

"Do either of you have any questions?" Autumn asked. "These are accredited results if you want to use them for legal purposes."

"No," Fiona said as she felt Marc stiffen at the word *legal*. "No questions. I just needed to know." *So I wouldn't be fighting for a dream that couldn't be.*

"Marc?" Autumn asked.

"It's all clear to me."

"Great. I have copies for each of you." Autumn

handed them envelopes from her folder. "And if any questions come up, you can call me."

Autumn was looking at Marc more than at her. She and Marc had grown up together. Autumn didn't know Fiona from anyone. Was her offer actually to support Marc against her if he decided he needed it?

But he didn't need it. All she was asking was to be part of her niece's life, on his terms. Fiona's thoughts went to Sunday dinner at the Delacroixs before Marc had made his announcement. Or was that really all she was asking?

Marc lifted his hand from hers, breaking her thought. They thanked Autumn, left her office and walked to the entryway of the building in silence—a silence that nagged at Fiona.

"Where do we go from here?" she asked.

Marc gave her a puzzled look as he held open the exit door for her. "Where we were going before."

She stepped out and a surprisingly mild winter breeze blew over her softly. It seemed as if she hadn't needed the DNA to prove Stella was her niece, to prove herself.

He fell in step with her as they walked to their vehicles. "As I said at dinner Sunday, we'll work with Renee and Noah, let Stella get to know you and tell Stella when we all feel she's ready."

Marc made it sound so simple. Was she overcomplicating things? Everything in life didn't have to be difficult.

"You're Claire's friend, my friend. We can include you in some family things so Stella can get used to you in those settings as well as through Bridges."

His slow smile encouraged her even more than his words had.

Marc had thought this out further than she had. She hadn't gotten beyond having the one last piece of proof. She hadn't allowed herself the hope to think seriously about how they were going to go forward or what she would have done if the testing had been less conclusive. But of course he had. He had more at stake than she did.

Or did he?

Fiona's hesitation to respond made the back of his neck prickle. "Hey, I have an idea," he said to fill the void. "Do you have plans for the rest of the afternoon and evening?"

"Not really, unless you count a trip to the laundromat as plans."

He laughed. "We could do that, or we could pick up Stella and go to the Paradox Lake General Store and get burgers."

Natalie and Connor would ask about the test results when he picked up Stella, and for some reason he wasn't ready to share the answer alone. Maybe because of Fiona's reaction to the results. He'd expected her to be elated. Instead, she'd been uncertain, closed in. They needed to present themselves as a team to his family, especially to his mother.

"Have you been there?" he asked. "The store has a small restaurant area."

"No."

His stomach muscles clenched when the silence between them passed the two-second mark. "Instead of going to the laundromat, you could throw your laundry in at my place to wash while we pick up Stella and to dry while we're eating."

She looked at him.

"That was weird, right?" he asked. So was his desperate need to keep her with him.

Fiona burst out laughing, making her copper curls dance around her lightly freckled face, drawing his attention to her dimples—so like his daughter's. A spot opened in his heart, a spot he'd kept tightly closed since Cate's death—one he wasn't ready to open.

"Yes, it's weird, and no, I haven't been there," Fiona said when she'd regained her voice. "You think it's a good idea, the three of us?"

He had no clue. He wasn't thinking. He was reacting. "Stella has to get used to you being a part of..." His lips started to say *my* before he corrected himself. "Her life, the family." Marc leaned against the side of her car while she unlocked it. "Come on. It'll be fun."

"All right," she relented. "Give me a time and directions, and I'll meet you there."

He pushed away from the car. "I'd like you to come with me to Nat and Connor's place to pick up Stella." He scratched the back of his neck. "So we can tell them the DNA results together."

"Do you think that's necessary?" Fiona clutched her keys. "At dinner, everyone but your mother seemed to accept me, or did I read them wrong?"

"No, they did." He fumbled for words to explain his need to have her with him and came up with none. "They'll be happy for you. I want you to see that." That was the part of his need he could grasp, anyway.

"All right. I'll follow you."

"They live in the house next to the church."

She nodded and slid into her car.

Twenty minutes later, Marc glanced in his rearview mirror to make sure Fiona had seen his turn signal before he turned onto Hazard Cove Road and into the parsonage driveway. He gave Fiona time to pull in behind him before he got out and waited for her.

"What a pretty house," she said when she joined him.

He looked at the two-story white clapboard house that looked like dozens of others in the area, including his parents' house.

"I love the big front porch and the gingerbread house bird feeder," she said, slowing her pace as they approached the porch stairs. Her gaze went to the Adirondack chairs set to look out over the lawn. "You know, I've never lived in a house. I mean a whole house."

Her words and wistful expression made Marc pause. He knew not every family in the area owned their homes, but when he was growing up here, at least, everyone he knew lived in a house. It wasn't until he'd gone away to college that he'd met people who'd grown up living in an apartment.

She smiled. "If the farm-to-table program takes off and is renewed next year, I'm going to look at houses, now that I have another reason to stay in the area."

"It's a good investment."

Fiona cocked her head.

"I can give you the name of the real estate agent who helped me find my rental house." Of course, her other reason to stay assumed La Table Frais would take off, too, and he and Stella would still be here next year.

"Are you two going to come in?" Pastor Connor stood inside the front screen door. "Or are you going to spend the afternoon examining the steps?"

"Get in here," Natalie said around her husband's shoulder. "Hi, Fiona."

Marc swept his hand forward, motioning Fiona to go ahead of him.

"Hi, Natalie, Pastor Connor," Fiona said. "I was admiring the house, and I love your bird feeder."

Connor pushed the door open for them, and Marc craned his neck to see around Fiona and Natalie, looking for Stella the minute he stepped inside. He didn't see her.

"Stella and Luc are at the dining room table coloring," Natalie said.

From the way she bit her bottom lip, Marc sensed another reason Natalie hadn't brought the kids in the room with her.

"I had to change Stella's clothes after her nap," Natalie said. "She had an accident, and it upset her."

"That hasn't happened in a long time."

"The poor little thing couldn't get her pants down fast enough. She has on a pair of Luc's jeans and undies. She was a little put out that he didn't have any with ponies or giraffes on them like she has."

"We'd better not go out for burgers." He shot Fiona an apologetic look.

"Have you made the appointment with the specialist?" Natalie touched her finger to her lips and glanced at Fiona, whose eyes widened.

"It's okay," he said to Fiona as much as to Natalie, "and yes, I made the appointment."

"Mommy, Stella took my crayon." Luc's voice came from the other room, interrupting the conversation before Marc could tell Fiona he'd fill her in later.

"I'll take care of it," Connor said.

"If Stella isn't feeling well and we aren't going out to eat, maybe I should go. I don't want to upset her."

Marc felt a pang of disappointment when Fiona turned to Natalie, not him, for direction. Or was it disappointment about not getting to spend the evening together?

"Wait, we need to tell Natalie the results first."

"Good news, I take it?"

"Yes, the DNA test showed an eighty-seven percent probability that Fiona is Stella's aunt."

"Wonderful. When Stella is older, she won't have to wonder about her birth mother—you can tell her." Natalie opened her arms. "Welcome to the family."

Marc watched Fiona step into Natalie's hug. He swallowed the bitter tang in his mouth. Now he was feeling jealous of his sister.

Fiona stepped out of Natalie's embrace, her eyes shiny. "Thank you." She turned to Marc. "You'll get back to me if you or your partners want any more changes in the contract I sent you, so I can finalize it and get to work on a plan?"

Marc had to think a second. Work. She was talking about work, distancing herself. "Right, I'll let you know as soon as I do."

"Bye."

The crunch of Fiona's footsteps on the stone driveway sounded through the screen.

"Do you think the testing is conclusive enough to sway Mom?" Natalie asked.

"She said something to you?"

"No, I'm going on the strange way she acted Sunday."

"It's going to have to be enough, because I'm not going to keep Fiona from Stella. I think it's important she be in Stella's life."

"And yours, big brother?"

"That question doesn't merit an answer." *Because the one that's front and center in my mind is all wrong, for so many reasons.*

Chapter Six

Looks like I have to reschedule our tour.

Fiona's heart sank when she read Marc's text. After the disappointment of having their burgers with Stella nixed on Wednesday, she'd been thrilled when he'd called her on Thursday and invited her to tour La Table Frais this morning.

Is Stella sick? Fiona texted back.

No. Mom. She can't pick her up from preschool. Are you free this afternoon?

Yeah, all I have is some paperwork, which I can do now.

Good. Meet me at the church about 12:30, after I pick Stella up from school. We'll all drive down to Glens Falls from there.

All? He must mean Stella, too. Fiona's heart lifted at the thought of the three of them together. She bit back the impulse to ask him in case she'd misunderstood. This *was* a business meeting. And she was happy enough to spend the afternoon with just Marc.

See you then, she answered.

After Marc's text, Fiona had trouble sitting still and concentrating on her work. But a few hours later, she was finished and headed up the sidewalk toward the church. The door to the hall opened as she approached it, and Marc stepped out with Stella holding his hand, dancing around beside him.

Fiona's breath caught at the sight of the tall dark-haired man in his businesslike trench coat and gray slacks, and the tiny little girl in her bright blue snow jacket and snowflake-patterned mittens and ski cap, red tresses curling up around the bottom of the hat. Marc waved when he spotted her, and Fiona got out of her car.

"Perfect timing," he called as he walked Stella over to her car. "I should have thought of this. Did you have lunch? Stella and I ate with her class."

"I'm good," Fiona said. The butterflies of anticipation in her stomach had taken care of any hunger she may have had. She dropped her gaze to Stella, who retreated behind Marc, and the butterflies disappeared to be replaced by a lead weight.

Marc gently moved Stella around him to face Fiona. "Sweetpea, you remember Fiona. She works with Daddy and Aunt Claire."

Fiona's heart constricted with the little girl's narrowing eyes.

"Feena played balloons."

"Yes, I did. I'm going to come with you and your daddy to see his restaurant."

"My daddy." Stella threw her arms around Marc's

leg as if she feared Fiona would take him away, and Marc tensed.

Fiona had no intention of coming between the father and daughter. Still, she couldn't shed the feeling that once again, she was on the outside looking in.

"Stella, we talked about this." Marc unwrapped Stella's arms and picked her up, putting her on eye level with Fiona. "Fiona is our friend. She came to Gammy and Papa's for Sunday dinner."

"No." Stella shook her head.

Fiona's insides clenched. This was a bad idea. She and Marc should have waited and met Monday morning without Stella.

"Luc's my friend," Stella said.

Fiona couldn't read the bright look that flashed on Marc's face when Stella spoke.

"We can have more than one friend," he said, before he motioned to Fiona. "My car's down the row to your left."

Stella scrunched her face, reminding Fiona so much of Mairi preparing to throw a fit that it hurt.

"I can drive my own car," Fiona said.

Marc followed her sideways glance at Stella. "No, let's go together."

Marc's insistence affected her in ways it shouldn't have. They were essentially testing the waters with Stella in a situation where Marc's business, not their new family relationship, was front and center. Or at least that's what Fiona had told herself repeatedly on the drive down from Willsboro.

Marc pressed his key fob to unlock his SUV and opened the back door. "I'll get Stella in her seat."

Fiona walked around to the passenger side and opened the door.

"Stella's seat," the little girl said as Marc fastened her in.

Fiona stifled a nervous giggle at Stella staking her territory. "I know. I'll sit up front with your daddy." She bit her lip, remembering Stella's earlier possessiveness.

"Daddy drive," Stella said as Marc climbed behind the wheel.

"Yes, it's your daddy's car."

"Stella and Daddy's car."

Marc smiled and turned on the engine. "Now that we have that all established, let's hit the road."

They were barely on the highway before Stella was fast asleep.

"Is this her usual nap time?" It was a safe icebreaker topic.

Marc's responding laugh had an edge to it. "Stella's nap time has devolved into whenever and wherever she runs out of steam. Thank you, preschool, for a busy morning." He tapped the steering wheel with his gloved finger. "Today was a bad idea, wasn't it?"

The note of uncertainty in his voice surprised her. Marc had struck her as a man who thought things out, then made a decision and went for it. She'd figured he had a reason for bringing Stella, beyond not wanting to cancel their meeting on short notice.

"We should have discussed getting together with Stella," he said. "Made a plan together. Although so far, it hasn't gone badly."

The right corner of his mouth tilted up, lifting Fiona's spirits with it.

"I had visions of trapping you in the car with a screaming Stella for an hour."

"I know what that's like."

Marc tilted his head and knitted his brow.

"My baby sister…" Fiona gripped the armrest with her right hand. Why had she said that? She never volunteered information about her family.

"Stella's birth mother?"

The impersonal phrasing raised Fiona's hackles. He could have used her sister's name. "No, not Mairi. We had a younger sister, Elsbeth. We called her Beth."

"Ah, the middle name on Stella's original birth certificate."

Fiona's throat clogged. "Yes, Mairi named her baby after both of us."

"Stella's middle name is Marie," Marc said.

Marie, Mary, Mairi. Fiona blinked at the almost painfully bright sun reflecting off the snow. She had to say something to end this conversation before Marc started asking more questions she'd rather not answer. She wanted him and his family to accept her, even to like her.

"I like that." *Marie—something from our family.*

"So what were you saying about your youngest sister?"

Had she really thought she could change the subject that easily? "Our mother had to take Beth to the UMV Cancer Center at the University of Vermont in Burlington. I remember her crying all the way there and sometimes back until she wore herself out." Fiona glanced over her shoulder at the sleeping Stella. "Beth didn't like riding in the car."

Who would, in their old car? It was either freezing in the winter because the heater didn't work right, or sweltering in the summer because it had no air conditioning. "The hour and a half drive seemed forever to Mairi and me."

Fiona rubbed her temples. *But, Lord, I gladly would*

have taken a hundred more of the head-splitting trips if only Mom hadn't given up on Beth, on all of us, in favor of her addiction.

"Did she make it?" Marc's voice was deep and low and touched her to her core.

"No, Beth died when she was three. Mairi was seven, and I was eleven."

"I'm sorry."

"It's okay. It was a long time ago." But talking about Beth made it seem like yesterday, which was one of the reasons she didn't talk about her or her family in general. Fiona wanted to live in the moment, not dwell on the past, chasing childhood fantasies. She was an adult now. She knew what she could control and what she shouldn't try to control, and she knew better than to want for anything more than her work and the financial security and personal satisfaction it provided.

"Mama," Stella cried out in her sleep.

Fiona jerked around, and Stella looked at her with wide, unseeing eyes.

"It's okay, baby," Marc soothed. "Daddy's here."

The little girl closed her eyes and stuck her thumb in her mouth.

Fiona faced front again, leaned back in her seat and stared out the windshield while her pulse worked itself down to normal. Her niece was icing on the cake of life to be savored when offered, but not Fiona's responsibility. Still, having talked about Beth, she had to ask.

"The other day, at Pastor Connor's, your sister asked whether you'd scheduled an appointment with a specialist." Fiona twisted her hands in her lap. "Is Stella okay?"

Marc flicked the windshield wipers on against the light snow that had begun. "She's fine." That's what he'd decided to think until he knew otherwise. "Her pediatrician said her growth was falling behind for her age and he wants to rule out any possible medical reason. That's all."

"I see."

She saw what? Marc focused his attention on the road as the snow picked up. It was enough that his mother and sisters were prodding him about Stella's stomachaches. Their former counselor had said the complaints were probably stress related, and he was working on that. He'd signed up for the adult Bridges Group. And so had Fiona.

"Was your sister Mairi petite, small as a child? Stella's new pediatrician asked me."

Fiona shook her head. "She was average, like me."

From what Marc had seen, there was nothing average about Fiona Bryce, looks or otherwise.

"But." Fiona hesitated. "Beth was always tiny."

Marc hit a patch of ice, and he hated to admit it, but he welcomed having something to focus on other than the thoughts building in the back of his mind. Stella was fine. "So Stella could be small for her age simply because of heredity."

"She could be."

Marc ignored the hint of doubt he thought he'd heard in Fiona's voice. "You haven't said anything about the email I sent you yesterday." *There. Business. A neutral subject.*

Relief matching his own spread across Fiona's face. "I agree with everything your partners had to say, especially their recommendation for joining the Chamber of Commerce and seeking a spot on the Farmer's Market Association board."

Of course, she'd jump on the two things he wasn't

one hundred percent behind. He didn't want to become too entrenched in local commitments because of the time involved, and because he was leaving his options open for returning downstate once the restaurant here was up and running.

"You disagree?" she asked. "Your expression."

"It's the time factor. With Stella. My partners don't get what's involved in being a single parent."

"I should have considered that. I had custody of Mairi when she was a teenager and I was at Cornell, after our mother died."

Another piece in the Fiona puzzle.

"And I should warn you," she said. "Teenagers are as time-consuming as toddlers, and share some other characteristics with them."

He laughed. "I'll keep that in mind."

"I still think you should come with me to one of the co-op meetings."

"Sure. Let me know when, and I'll put you on my calendar." He stuttered. "*It* on my calendar." He didn't have to say that. She knew what he meant.

"Daddy."

"Hey, sweetpea. Did you have a good nap?"

"No nap."

Fiona almost succeeded at suppressing her laugh.

"I want juice."

He jerked back in his seat at his daughter's use of *I*, garnering a quizzical look from Fiona. "We're almost to the restaurant. I can get your juice when we stop."

"Feena no juice."

"Stella, what did D—" he caught himself "—I tell you at lunch about sharing?" Not referring to himself as Daddy might help correct Stella's way of speaking.

Stella huffed, reminding him of Cate on the too-often occasions he'd called to say he'd be working late, before he'd started texting instead.

"Stella shares with Mia at school."

Guilt melded with letdown when his daughter used her name again, rather than *I*. He'd tried. "Yes, but not just with Mia and the other kids at school."

"It's okay." Fiona jumped in. "I brought water."

She probably thought she was helping. But if he and Fiona were going to be raising Stella together… He put a halt to that out-of-the-blue thought. They weren't raising Stella together any more than he and any of his three sisters were. Fiona was Stella's aunt, which was all she'd asked to be, and his business associate. He shouldn't be thinking of her in any other way—but he did, all too often.

"See? Feena no juice."

He rolled his shoulders against the back of his seat. Maybe preschool hadn't been such a great idea. Where else could this attitude be coming from? His control of Stella was slipping away. Too many outside factors were weighing in—school and his family, among others.

"If you want a drink now, I'll share my water with you," Fiona offered.

Fiona, too. If Fiona was going to be part of his daughter's life, the two of them needed to be on the same page where Stella was concerned.

"No fank you," Stella said.

Marc and Fiona burst into laughter, ramping down his tension.

"Here we are," he said as he recovered and pulled his vehicle up the snow-covered drive.

"Wow!" Fiona said when the tan cut-stone building came into view. "Not what I expected. Very impressive, like one of the Great Camps of the Gilded Era."

"It's a scaled-down near replica of one, built by someone who had not quite as much money," Marc said, allowing himself some pride in having been the one who'd found the building. "When the weather permits, we'll be painting the wooden window and porch trim the original salmon color."

"Nice and not what I expected, considering where you're coming from."

Marc brought the SUV to a stop by the front door. Fiona's words rubbed him. He'd told her it was a historic camp. What had she expected?

"I was seeing something sleek, chrome and glass. Frank Lloyd Wright-ish."

"Have you been to our New York restaurant?"

"No."

"Because you just described it."

"Ha, so I was sort of right."

"Daddy, juice."

"I'll get it," he said, glad for the distraction to give him time to digest Fiona's perception of who he was. He jumped out, his boots sinking into the knee-high snow piled by the driveway. He opened the back door of the car and retrieved the juice boxes he had stashed in a bag on the floor. "Here you go." Marc stuck a straw in the juice box and handed it to Stella.

Fiona waited for him in front of the SUV while he unbuckled Stella and carried her over. A narrow, shoveled path led to the front door of the restaurant.

"The contractor has been using the back door." Marc pointed toward the back of the building to a tall stone arch over the driveway. "But I want you to see the dining room first."

He led Fiona up the steps to the covered porch, unlocked and pushed open the heavy oak door. He held the pine-framed screen door for Fiona.

"It's gorgeous," she said even before she was all the way into the dining room.

"Make up for the lack of chrome and glass?"

"Cut me some slack," she said. "I came across the 'Up and Coming in New York Cuisine' profile online when I was researching your business."

Marc clenched his jaw. That article had come out just before his career and single-parent balance had imploded. He'd suspected that his partners had been behind it, as an encouraging boost, but had never asked. Fiona was right. He had been chrome and glass. The glass had shattered and left him a tarnished chrome shell.

"Down," Stella insisted.

Marc placed her on the floor, removed her mittens and cap and unzipped her coat. Stella handed him her juice box and tugged at a sleeve to take her coat off.

"It's cold in here. We're going to leave our coats on."

Fiona removed her gloves and hat, stuck them in the bag she had slung over her shoulder and unzipped her coat. Stella eyed her to see if she was going to take it off. Satisfied that Fiona wasn't, Stella held her hand up for her juice box, grabbed it from Marc and took off across the room toward the mammoth stone fireplace that was the focal point of the room.

"Fire!" Stella shouted.

Marc and Fiona followed at a more leisurely pace.

"You might not have noticed when you were at the house, but my parents have a woodstove insert in the front room fireplace. Stella is fascinated by the flames."

Fiona gripped the strap of her bag and pressed her lips together.

He crossed his arms across his chest. "She knows the stove is hot and not to touch it." Marc unfolded his arms and ruffled Stella's curls. "No fire today. The man has to come and clean the chimney before we can light a fire."

Stella stuck out her bottom lip and Marc held his breath, waiting. A mix of helplessness and frustration filled him that he couldn't better anticipate and defuse the triggers to his daughter's outbursts. Or, as he'd heard from one of the downstate babysitters, was Stella just plain spoiled?

"Yo, Marc." Sean, one of the construction crew, a guy he'd played baseball with in high school, walked in from the kitchen, diverting Stella's attention and drawing Fiona's.

Marc eyed the guy's muscle shirt and swagger as he strode toward him.

"We've got a problem. The chief wants you to come and take a look. Black mold behind the old freezer unit. We may need to rip out the whole wall and replace it."

"All right. Stella, you need to stay with Fiona."

Fiona offered her hand to Stella. "Let's go look out the window at the birds at the bird feeder while Daddy works."

He gave Fiona a thumbs-up just before Stella let go with a loud, "No, go with Daddy!"

"You have to stay with Fiona. It's dangerous, like the fire." He didn't need her breathing in the mold the crew had uncovered.

"No fire today," Stella said. "Go with Daddy."

He wasn't going to stand here in front of Sean and Fiona and argue with a two-year-old. Marc nodded at Fiona. She caught his message and bent to pick up Stella. The little girl raced across the short distance between her and Marc, but not before he'd caught the pain on Fiona's face.

"Hey, cutie, what's your name?" The workman scooped her up and handed Marc a facemask. "I've got this. I have one at home her size."

Stella tilted her face to Marc. She'd run away from Fiona, but seemed to be fine with a strange man picking her up, despite him reading her a stranger-danger storybook on a regular basis. On a scale of difficulty, parenting blew anything else he'd done out of the water.

"It's okay," he said. "He's Sean, my work friend."

"Like Feena?"

Not at all. "Something like that," Marc said and headed to the kitchen.

Fifteen minutes later, he returned to the dining room. Fiona, Stella and the workman were at the far window by the bird feeder chatting away like old friends. Marc ground his molars. He modulated his steps and fought the urge to stomp across the room and claim his girls.

"What's the verdict?" Sean asked.

"The wall has to come down."

"I'll get back to work, then. Nice meeting you, Fiona, Stella."

"You, too," Fiona said.

Was it his out-of-control imagination, or did Fiona's gaze linger on the other man as he walked away? And what if it did? Why should he care if Fiona was flirting with Sean? Except Sean was married. Marc clenched and unclenched his fists. They had to get out of here. He was going crazy.

"Sorry I can't show you the kitchen."

"I understand," Fiona said. "We covered all of our business already on the drive down."

That's right. This was business. Although he had

wanted Fiona to see his self-designed kitchen setup. "Let's head back. Come on, Stella." He held out her hat and mittens.

"Bye-bye, birdies," she said.

He squatted to put Stella's mitten on her, and the sound of male voices drifted in from the kitchen. Marc straightened to face Fiona. "I was thinking that you might want to come with us to Stella's appointment with the gastroenterologist. Family history and all that. And we need to schedule that one-on-one session with Noah." He scuffed his toe against the polished wood floor. "You know, the Bridges thing."

Fiona's smile shot right through him. "Yes, I'd like to."

There. He struck his claim. But to what exactly was another question.

Chapter Seven

Fiona rose and went out to the medical center hallway for a second drink of water. Where were Marc and Stella? The only contact she'd had with Marc the past week was his text to confirm she was coming to Stella's appointment and her response that she'd meet him here. It didn't make sense for him to go out of his way to pick her up at the farm.

Fiona had thought about attending service at Hazardtown Community Church yesterday, but that had somehow struck her as stalker-ish. She'd tried the Stone Church in Schroon Lake instead and, while it hadn't felt like a good fit, simply hearing God's words had made her less apprehensive about Stella's appointment this afternoon.

She returned to the waiting room and rifled through the folder of medical records she'd brought—Mairi's childhood ones from when she had custody of her and the ones Fiona had received from Autumn Hanlon at the birthing center. Most likely overkill, but she liked to be prepared, not that she ever felt fully prepared when dealing with Marc and Stella.

"Hey, been waiting long?"

Fiona slapped the folder shut. "Hi, Marc, Stella."

The little girl had no reaction to her greeting, which Fiona took as a good thing. "I've been here a few minutes. I overestimated the time it would take to drive from the office."

"Never a bad idea with the winter weather here. I'll go check Stella in. Stay here with Fiona," he said to his daughter.

"'Kay." Stella crawled up on the chair next to Fiona. Another good sign.

The little girl swung her feet back and forth. "Don't cry, and Feena will get a good girl prize."

Fiona wasn't sure what Stella meant, but Stella talking to her with no prompting warmed her to the core.

Marc folded his tall frame into the chair on Stella's other side. "Her pediatrician gave her a coloring book after her exam."

"Stella colors at school, for Daddy. Luc scribbles, breaks crayons. Aunt Dee says no."

"My oldest sister, Andie," Marc explained.

Stella and Marc's reminders of their family pushed Fiona to the outside of the circle of intimacy she'd felt around the three of them. *No*, she admonished herself, *you're part of Stella's family, too.*

"Stella Delacroix," a nurse called from the doorway to the exam rooms. The three of them rose and followed the nurse. She took Stella's vital signs and said the doctor would be with them in a minute.

A knock on the door signaled his arrival. "Hello, Mr. and Mrs. Delacroix, Stella, I'm Dr. Franklin."

"Marc," he extended his hand, "and this is a family friend, Fiona Bryce. I'm a widower."

Dr. Franklin glanced from Stella to Fiona. "Sorry for my presumption. And how are you, Stella?"

"Almost free," she answered, misunderstanding his question and holding up three fingers.

Dr. Franklin laughed and explained to Stella in children's terms what he was going to do in his exam.

"Great job," he said when he finished. "Would you like to go look at the fish in the waiting room with my nurse while I talk with your daddy and Fiona? My nurse has something for you," Dr. Franklin added.

"A good girl prize! 'Kay, Daddy?"

Fiona released the breath she hadn't realized she was holding.

"Sure." Marc visibly relaxed, an action the doctor appeared to pick up on.

"We can talk in my office. The nurses' station is on the way."

Marc lifted Stella from the exam table and they followed the doctor into the hall.

"Sonja," he said to the nurse who'd taken Stella's vitals, "Stella would like to go see my fish, and I told her you would have something for her."

"Right. Come on, Stella. We have a new fish that likes to hide in the rocks. Let's see if we can find him."

Stella looked up at Marc.

"Go ahead, sweetpea."

Fiona's heart clenched at how willingly the little girl went with the nurse, compared to her reaction to staying with Fiona at Marc's restaurant.

Marc leaned toward her, his warm breath tickling her ear. "For whatever reason, she's more comfortable with older women."

Had she been that transparent? Fiona thought she had better control of her emotions than that.

They followed the doctor to his office and sat in the

two chairs facing his desk. Fiona placed her folder on the desk.

Marc eyed it and cleared his throat. "Before you start, I…we need to share a few family details. Stella is adopted. Fiona is her birth mother's sister. She…we only recently learned that. Fiona can tell you her family history." His words seemed to trip over each other.

"Good. From my exam and your pediatricians' records, I have some questions. Do you know of any instances of IBS or Crohn's disease in the immediate family?"

Fiona froze.

"No, not that I know of," Marc answered.

"My family has a history." The words scraped across Fiona's vocal chords.

Dr. Franklin picked up a pen. "IBS or Crohn's?"

"Crohn's."

The doctor made a note. "There's not an absolute proven hereditary correlation, but Crohn's disease appears to run in some families. Stella's birth mother?"

"No, our younger sister."

"Adult or child onset?" the doctor asked.

"Child."

An arctic chill radiated from Marc.

"She has it successfully managed?" Dr. Franklin asked.

"No. I mean, she died when she was about Stella's age, from colon cancer."

"Are you saying Stella has Crohn's disease?" Marc interrupted. He stopped and dropped his hands to his lap.

Without thinking, Fiona reached over and covered his hand with hers, surprised when he didn't pull away.

"My wife, Cate, died of bone cancer when Stella was eighteen months old."

"The risk of colorectal cancer in young children is very low, unless inflammation goes unmanaged and the entire colon becomes affected," Dr. Franklin reassured him.

Tears moistened Fiona's eyes. She'd been only a child herself, but… "My mother didn't do a good job of following the instructions Beth's doctors had given her."

The two men stared at her.

"I read them," Fiona said. "I probably understood them as much as my mother did." *Even in her lucid moments.* "I did what I could to help."

Dr. Franklin's expression turned compassionate, and Fiona squirmed. What did it matter if her words had given the doctor, or even Marc, insight into where she'd come from? That was the past. She was here today for Stella.

"I haven't made a diagnosis," the doctor continued. "I'm still gathering information and will want to run some tests once I look at the results of the bloodwork I've ordered." He explained the possible tests.

When the doctor had finished, Marc glanced down at Fiona's hand on his and pulled it—and the warmth they'd shared—away.

"I want you to schedule an appointment to bring Stella back in two weeks," Dr. Franklin said. "Until then, keep a journal of what she eats and note any complaints of stomach discomfort. Will that be a problem at daycare?"

"No, she's usually with me or my mother for lunch, and my sister is her teacher at preschool." Marc drew his lips into a grim line. That was assuming Mom took his directions from Dr. Franklin seriously. She had her own ways of doing things and might treat the food diary as unnecessary.

"I'm advising against either of you doing too much online research on IBS and Crohn's until we have a diagnosis, but if you feel compelled to, stick with the Crohn's and Colitis Foundation and Mayo Clinic."

The doctor scratched the websites on a Post-it note that Marc stuffed in the pocket of his shirt.

"I'm familiar with both of the sites," Fiona said when Dr. Franklin reached for another Post-it.

Of course she was. He should be thankful for Fiona's input about her family's medical history. But after what Cate went through, the story Fiona had shared about her youngest sister just plain scared him, despite the reassurance Dr. Franklin had given him.

He and Fiona walked back to the waiting room in silence.

"Daddy!" Stella called when they reached the waiting room doorway. "We found the fish. See." She pointed at a blue-gray angelfish. "He looks like the rock."

Marc bent to Stella's level and squinted at the aquarium. "So he does."

"And I got 'nother coloring book. Luc no scribble." Stella shook her head emphatically.

"Nice," Marc said. "But remember what I said the other day about sharing."

Stella huffed. "'Kay."

"I'm going to head back to work," Fiona said. "See you Thursday evening."

Marc's mind blanked. Thursday evening was the Twenty-/Thirtysomethings regular meeting at church, but neither of them belonged, and he didn't remember making any plans to go.

"The meeting with Noah," she prompted. "Bridges."

"Right. See you then."

Marc watched Fiona leave and pasted a smile on his face for his daughter. At the moment, all he wanted to do was scoop up Stella, take her home and never let go. He gazed down at her studying the fish again, his heart nearly bursting.

Lord, please. I'm not strong enough to go through it again. Not with my baby.

Stella wasn't Beth. Fiona had told herself that a thousand times since Tuesday. But it hadn't entirely relieved the sick feeling in her stomach. Rationally, she knew that her mother's haphazard care of Beth was partially responsible for the deterioration in her baby sister's health, and she knew Marc would do anything for Stella. Still, a part of her wondered why he hadn't questioned the little girl's stomachaches earlier, and she answered herself—fairly or unfairly—that he'd simply been too wrapped up in his work.

Fiona pulled open the door to the building in Elizabethtown where the Christian Action Coalition had its offices. It probably would have made sense for her and Marc to drive up together, but he hadn't offered. He hadn't contacted her at all since Stella's doctor's appointment. Not that there was any reason he should have. *Except to reassure me about my place in Stella's life.* She wrinkled her nose. Fixating on Dr. Franklin's concerns had opened her old longing-to-belong wounds that she'd worked so hard to close.

Fiona quickly found the director's office and went in.

"Hi," Noah said. "You're the first to arrive."

"Hi." Fiona knew that. It's what she'd planned, after the discomfort of arriving last at the group meeting.

She'd checked the parking lot for Marc's SUV when she'd arrived.

"Take your coat off and join me." He rose from his desk and motioned first to a coatrack by the door and then to a couch and two chairs positioned in a horseshoe around a low table. "Would you like a cup of coffee while we wait for Marc?"

"No, thanks." She didn't need anything to add to her jitters.

"So how's it going?" he asked after she'd settled into one of the chairs.

"With Stella?" she asked.

"Or in general." He smiled.

Noah was obviously trying to make her feel more comfortable. But she wasn't comfortable, and would probably be even less so once Marc arrived.

"Work's good." She grasped onto the subject she felt most grounded in.

"You're with the Willsboro farm, right?"

"Yes, the new farm-to-table program." She searched for something else to say. "Marc and his partners are my first clients." For all of the other things she could have told Noah about her job, the reference to Marc just flowed out.

"Interesting."

She cocked her head toward him. Was he psychoanalyzing her? She'd certainly had enough experience with various school counselors over the years that she should know.

Noah sat calmly in the other chair.

"Marc showed me his restaurant the other week," she said when the silence grew too long for her. "We took Stella with us."

"And how did that work out?"

He *was* analyzing her. She checked the clock to see how close it was to seven. Six fifty-eight.

"So-so. Marc had to check out a problem the renovation contractor had found in the kitchen and needed Stella to stay in the dining room with me. She didn't want to."

"I see."

Fiona gritted her teeth and checked the clock again. She'd found the Bridges children's group activity valuable but was reassessing her agreement to participate in the adult group.

"Hey, sorry I'm late." Marc walked in and slipped off his coat.

His Oxford dress shirt and sharply creased slacks made her feel rumpled in the slacks and sweater she'd worn to work. While it hadn't made sense for her to drive home to Ticonderoga from work and back north to Elizabethtown, she could have brought a fresh outfit. She shook off a vision of herself in ill-fitting, thrift-shop clothes, sitting in the guidance counselor's office on her first day at the last high school she'd attended. She straightened in her seat. She wasn't that poor little Bryce girl anymore.

"No problem. It gave me a few minutes to get to know Fiona. I have to admit that I have quite a bit of backstory on you from your sister."

"Renee?" Marc laughed. "Only believe half of what any of my siblings say about each other—good or bad."

Fiona wondered if Noah had caught the edge on Marc's laugh. Or had she imagined it? He assessed the sitting arrangement and settled on the couch, his only option. Fiona resisted the inexplicable urge she had to join him.

"Fiona was telling me about you and her and Stella visiting your new restaurant."

Marc rubbed his chin. "Yeah, that didn't go as well as I'd hoped."

"Fiona said Stella was reluctant to stay with her."

"Not as much as she could have been. She didn't throw a fit or anything."

"She's done that before?" Noah asked.

"Unfortunately." Marc rubbed the back of his neck. "Stella seems to be comfortable only with older women and my sisters. What bothered me was that Stella went right to one of the construction workers." Marc's face hardened.

That had bothered her, too, but she couldn't fathom why it would have bothered Marc.

"I've tried to teach her stranger danger."

"You were there. I'm sure she felt safe," Noah said.

But not safe with me. Fiona studied her hands in her lap.

"Back to Stella not wanting to stay with Fiona. The restaurant visit was, what, the third time Stella has been with Fiona?"

Marc's eyes narrowed, and Fiona sank back in her chair.

"Renee said you introduced Fiona to all of your family a couple weeks ago."

"Did she also tell you that my mother was not receptive?"

Fiona caught the sharp edge in Marc's response and sank farther into the chair.

"She did. How do each of you feel about that?" Noah asked.

Fiona opened her mouth to answer, but Marc stopped her by raising his hands to Noah, palms out.

"Wait a minute. I thought the purpose of the adult group, of our meeting with you, was to help us develop strategies for working together to help Stella adjust to losing her mother, moving here and, on top of all of that, having an aunt appear whom no one knew about. Let's drop the feelings stuff and cut to the chase. My hopes are that we can leave tonight with a plan to introduce Fiona to Stella as her aunt sooner rather than later."

"What's your hurry?" Noah asked.

"Stella said something to my mother when she was watching her today about Fiona not being her aunt. I don't know where Stella picked that up. I'm not even sure she knows exactly what an aunt is, only that she has several. Mom didn't disagree. She said she didn't want to confuse Stella, which I can appreciate." He stopped and took a deep breath.

"But your mother's still not convinced, even by the DNA test," Fiona finished for him.

"No." Marc turned to Noah. "As to how I feel about Mom—confused. It's totally out of character for her to refuse to accept Fiona despite the proof. Everyone else in the family has."

Fiona warmed at Marc's defense of her.

"This is good," Noah said. "You've targeted a major goal. I'm going to suggest a modification. Rather than focusing on Fiona being Stella's aunt, bring Fiona into the family without a label. Marc has a good point about the possibility of Stella not fully understanding family connections. Now, fill me in on Dr. Franklin."

Marc told him about Stella's checkup and appointment with Dr. Franklin.

"So you may have a health issue thrown in with our other challenges."

"Not necessarily," Marc corrected Noah. "The counselor I took Stella to downstate said her stomachaches could be triggered by the stress of dealing with the loss of her mother. Her pediatrician there wasn't concerned about her growth development—at least at the couple of checkups I took her to after… That's something Cate had always handled."

Fiona's stomach twisted in a sharp spasm. Was he as much in denial about the possibility that Stella had a medical condition as his mother was about her being Stella's aunt?

"All right," Noah said. "Where do you go from here?"

Marc bristled. "If I knew I wouldn't be here."

Fiona pulled together her confident, professional persona, even if it was a facade at the moment. "We need to talk with Mrs. Delacroix together, and then plan more activities with all of us and Stella to help her get used to me being part of her family."

"What do you suggest?" Noah looked from her to Marc.

Marc stretched his legs out under the table. "I could make dinner for her and Dad at my place."

An offhand remark Claire had made one day at work about never turning down an invitation to a meal cooked by Marc ran through Fiona's head. It wasn't that she didn't want him to cook dinner for her, but… "I'm not sure. I don't think Stella should be there because we'll be talking about her."

Marc grimaced. "We could make it lunch on a day Natalie could take her after school, if you're able to get time off work."

His reply almost sounded like a challenge as to whether she would put work ahead of Stella. "I could do that."

"Sounds good. We've made real progress," Noah said. "Should we call it a night?"

"Fine by me," Marc said, rising before he finished speaking.

Fiona nodded, mulling over what progress Noah had thought they'd made.

"See you at the next group meeting," Noah said as Marc opened the door for Fiona. "You have my number if you need to meet again before then."

"Like that's going to happen," Marc muttered under his breath once the door was firmly closed behind them.

Fiona scratched her cheek. She had no idea where Marc's animosity was coming from.

"We should have met by ourselves for all the help Noah was." Marc tugged on his ski cap. "Mom isn't going to like this. Despite Renee's vocation, she isn't a fan of counseling, taking family matters outside of the family."

Ah. So that's where it had come from.

He pushed open the outside door. "We may be better off waiting for Mom to come around on her own."

Fiona passed by him and turned, blocking Marc's way. "No, we need to have that lunch. Your mother doesn't have to like it. Nor does she have to like me. But she does need to accept the reality that I intend to be involved in Stella's life."

For the first time since he'd moved back north, Marc was questioning his choice—really questioning it. He turned down the flame under his Irish stew and stirred it. His life had gotten out of control downstate, and it seemed to be careening in the same direction here.

He'd totally lost control of the meeting with Noah. His mother had given him a tight-lipped *yes* to his lunch invitation when he'd said Fiona was joining. Stella's old pediatrician hadn't had the concerns the doctors here had. He'd pressed like a maniac for anything that might have put Cate's cancer in remission and that hadn't gotten them anywhere. Now Stella...

He dropped the lid on the Dutch oven. He'd like to lay all of the blame on Fiona's appearance in their lives and simply wish her away. Except that he liked her. Yeah, he had to admit it. He liked being around her, having her as part of the family. And whether Fiona cared or not, he wanted his mother to like her.

A knock and the sound of the kitchen door opening behind him put a stop to the direction of those thoughts.

"Hi," his mother said, walking in with a covered plate. "I brought some of the apple crisp with walnuts that Stella likes."

Marc looked behind his mother for his father. "Where's Dad?"

"He and Paul had a problem with the milking machine this morning, so he had to stay and finish."

"It must have been some problem if they're still milking at noon." Or his father had dragged it out so he could avoid the impending conflict. Lunch was all ready. Maybe he should volunteer to go help them.

"That and he had a feed delivery this morning that Paul had to unload."

"Dad's loss. I made Irish stew for him."

She took off her coat and boots and hung her coat on one of the hooks beside the door. "I'd expected you to make something more impressive. For Fiona."

He stopped just short of slapping his palm on the countertop next to him. "Mom, this isn't like you. What do you have against Fiona? You haven't even given yourself a chance to get to know her. If you did, you'd

"FAST FIVE" READER SURVEY

Your participation entitles you to:
✳ 4 Thank-You Gifts Worth Over $20!

Complete the survey in minutes.

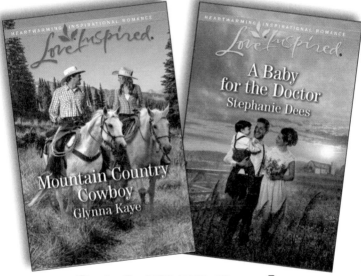

Get 2 FREE Books

Your Thank-You Gifts include **2 FREE BOOKS** and **2 MYSTERY GIFTS**. There's no obligation to purchase anything!

See inside for details.

Please help make our
"Fast Five" Reader Survey
a success!

Dear Reader,

Since you are a lover of our books, your opinions are important to us... and so is your time.

That's why we made sure your **"FAST FIVE" READER SURVEY** can be completed in just a few minutes. Your answers to the five questions will help us remain at the forefront of women's fiction.

And, as a thank-you for participating, we'd like to send you **4 FREE THANK-YOU GIFTS!**

Enjoy your gifts with our appreciation,

Pam Powers

To get your
4 FREE THANK-YOU GIFTS:

✳ Quickly complete the "Fast Five" Reader Survey
and return the insert.

▼ DETACH AND MAIL CARD TODAY! ▼

"FAST FIVE" READER SURVEY

1 Do you sometimes read a book a second or third time? ○ Yes ○ No

2 Do you often choose reading over other forms of entertainment such as television? ○ Yes ○ No

3 When you were a child, did someone regularly read aloud to you? ○ Yes ○ No

4 Do you sometimes take a book with you when you travel outside the home? ○ Yes ○ No

5 In addition to books, do you regularly read newspapers and magazines? ○ Yes ○ No

YES! I have completed the above Reader Survey. Please send me my 4 FREE GIFTS (gifts worth over $20 retail). I understand that I am under no obligation to buy anything, as explained on the back of this card.

❑ I prefer the regular-print edition
105/305 IDL GMVV

❑ I prefer the larger-print edition
122/322 IDL GMVV

FIRST NAME	LAST NAME

| ADDRESS |

| APT.# | CITY |

| STATE/PROV. | ZIP/POSTAL CODE |

like her. Natalie and Connor do, Renee does, and Claire does. And she works with her every day." He didn't mention his own feelings toward her, and the omission hung between them.

Marc's mother placed the apple crisp in his refrigerator and then faced him. "I only want your happiness."

Before Marc could begin to try to interpret that, the front doorbell rang. "That must be Fiona." He left his mother in the kitchen.

"Hi," he said, holding the door for her. "Let me take your coat."

"Thanks." She stomped the bit of snow off her low-cut leather boots and wiped her feet on the mat.

"I left my shoes at work," she apologized.

"Your boots are fine. The rug in here is mud-brown anyway."

He followed Fiona's gaze to the rug, his face heating when he caught the corners of her mouth turning up.

She removed her coat, her cold fingers brushing his warm ones as he took it from her. Marc resisted the impulse to rub her hands between his to warm them up.

"You should have worn gloves." What was wrong with his mouth? She was an adult; she knew when to wear gloves. He sounded like he was talking to Stella.

She laughed. "I have a pair in my pockets. What smells so wonderful?"

"That would be my Irish stew, and thanks."

Her expression sobered. "I saw the car in the driveway. Your parents are here?"

"Only Mom. Dad had a problem with the milking equipment and couldn't come."

"Oh."

"It's probably better that it's just the three of us." And if she believed that, he had a bridge to sell her. He'd invited his dad for a little more testosterone against the two women. He had a feeling that if she wanted to, Fiona could match his mother inch for inch, digging in her heels.

"The kitchen is this way. Everything is ready. Mom brought an extra dessert." As if the tiramisu he'd made last night—because Fiona had said she liked it—wasn't enough.

"Here you are," his mother said when they walked in.

Marc hoped Fiona hadn't caught the false brightness he'd heard in his mother's voice. But the frozen smile on Fiona's face said otherwise.

"I knew you wouldn't mind. I tasted the stew and added more salt and pepper."

He minded. As good a cook as his mother was, he was the professional, and he'd long thought she was heavy-handed on the salt and pepper and too sparse on more subtle spices.

"As I told Marc in the other room, it smells wonderful." Fiona rested her hands on the back of one of the chairs. "I can't wait to taste it. Claire told me that if Marc ever offered to cook for me, I was *not* to turn him down."

"Then I'll set the table," his mother said.

"Mom, sit. Please. This is my gig."

Marc stepped past her to the stove. He opened the oven for the crusty bread he'd baked last night that was warming, thankful for the blast of hot air to hide any flush of irritation on his face.

"Mmm, that smells as yummy as the stew."

He closed the oven and saw that Fiona had taken the seat across the table from the stove. Marc placed the bread on the table and removed the extra place setting at the far end across from his mother, leaving the other one beside her for him. He followed the bread with the pot of stew and pulled out his chair. "Go ahead, dig in."

His heartbeat stalled as Fiona and his mother looked at each other. Fiona reached for the stew ladle at the same time his mother lifted her hand to do the same. Fiona grasped the ladle and scooped a generous serving into her bowl.

Good girl. He should have known his mother wouldn't intimidate Fiona.

"I can't wait to taste this." Fiona turned the ladle toward his mother, who put a half scoop in her bowl before handing it to Marc.

"Would you say grace," his mother said, more a direction than a question.

He bowed his head. "Lord, we are grateful for this food and the opportunity to further welcome Fiona into our family."

When he lifted his head, his mother curled her lips in and released them. "I know why you invited me to lunch."

Marc tore the end piece off the loaf of bread and slapped on a knife full of butter.

His mother made a noise in the back of her throat. "I apologize for the rude way I've been acting, Fiona, Marc."

His gaze went to Fiona.

"Apology accepted," she said, a shadow he could only describe as longing passing over her face.

Marc bit into the crust of his bread, not feeling as gracious.

"Wait." His mother raised her hand. "I want to explain, so you understand my rudeness before you forgive it."

He chewed the bread slowly. This sounded more like the mother he knew.

"My sister, your aunt Margarette, and her husband adopted a baby girl a couple years after they married."

Fiona stiffened, and Marc stopped chewing, the bites he'd swallowed congealing in his stomach. Aunt Margarette and Uncle Ed didn't have a daughter, only a son.

"Days before the adoption was to be finalized, but within the legal time frame, the birth mother changed her mind. Margarette was devastated. She had to be treated for severe depression, and it was nearly ten years before they adopted your cousin Greg. I couldn't bear for Marc, for all of us, to go through that kind of pain."

"I wouldn't do that," Fiona said. "I told Marc I wouldn't."

He reached for his mother's hand and squeezed it. "And I told you my lawyer said Fiona has no standing to do that." His words sounded flat against Fiona's heartfelt ones.

"I was still afraid. You're a parent. You understand, and Fiona, Marc said you had custody of your sister after your mother died."

Fiona nodded, her expression open.

"I do understand, Mom." Yet he was having trouble giving his mother's apology the simple acceptance Fiona had seemed to.

"Well, I'm glad to have that out in the open. Isn't the stew fabulous?" his mother asked.

"Absolutely, as is the bread." The two women continued chatting in a polite manner.

Marc stared at his bowl. *That's it? We're all good now?*

After dessert with coffee, and after his mother had packed up several helpings of her apple crisp for Fiona to take home, Marc watched the two women walk to their cars like old friends. He sighed. Wasn't this what he wanted? For his mother to accept Fiona as one of the family?

He turned from the window in disgust. Lunch hadn't helped him gain any control. Just the opposite. Now, he was begrudging his mother the smiles and ease Fiona had for her. He was as bad as Stella had been about her new coloring book. He didn't want to share Fiona.

Chapter Eight

Fiona heard footsteps on the stairs leading up to her apartment. She'd been trying to keep an eye and an ear out for Marc, so he wouldn't have to come up, but her phone had rung with a call from someone offering her a student loan consolidation deal on student loans she didn't have, and she'd missed hearing his car pull into the driveway. The Bridges program had scheduled an afternoon of sledding for the families in Stella's group. This sort of activity seemed like a good way to get together with Marc and Stella, in line with what they'd talked about with Noah.

She answered the door on the first knock. "Sorry, I tried to listen for your car so you wouldn't have to come up." Fiona nodded at Stella.

"No problem. Stella wanted to see your house."

Fiona ran her finger under the scarf she'd tied securely around the collar of her jacket. Did that mean Stella wanted to see her?

"Feena's house." Stella pushed against Marc's chest to get down.

He placed her on the floor. The little girl took a few

steps, touched the couch and said, "Feena's couch," before moving on to touch the TV stand. "Feena's TV."

"Yes." Fiona laughed, as much from the joy of Stella at ease here as from her niece's overall cuteness.

Stella spun around. "Feena sleep?"

"Yes, I have a bedroom." Fiona pointed to a closed door, which Stella made a beeline for.

"Whoa, sweetpea. We came to pick Fiona up to go sledding, not to move in."

"'Kay."

"Maybe you could come over some other time and we could watch a video," Fiona said.

"Frozen?"

The way the little girl's face lit up warmed Fiona enough that she doubted she'd be cold during the sledding.

"But Daddy's tired of *Frozen*," Stella said sadly.

Marc shrugged. "What can I say? It's a little girly for me. But maybe we can come over sometime. I can cook us dinner or lunch while you girls watch the movie."

Fiona had been thinking along the lines of having just Stella over. But Marc would be a welcome addition. She suddenly felt the full impact of standing inside too long in her down jacket. *A welcome addition to make Stella feel more secure*, she told herself.

Marc removed his ski cap, ran his hand over his hair and replaced it. "We'd better get going. We don't want to miss out on the fun."

Stella raced back to him and lifted her arms. Once Marc had picked her up, she motioned to Fiona. "Feena, come. Sledding."

Fiona's heart swelled. Stella definitely seemed more comfortable with her today.

"I'm ready," she said, following Marc to the door. She stopped on the first step to turn and lock the door.

"Feena," Stella called again.

Fiona pressed her hand to her heart and listened to Marc's footsteps on the stairs. "I'm coming. I had to lock the door." She turned to see Marc and Stella reaching the bottom step, the little girl's wide smile a beacon to her.

Marc leaned against the door to hold it open for her and shifted Stella to his left hip. So she'd have to brush by the little girl rather than him?

"Boggan," Stella shouted and pointed at the rack on top of Marc's SUV.

"I see you've come prepared."

Marc stepped away and let the outer door slam shut, shifting Stella again as if to keep her as a buffer between them.

"The toboggan," Fiona said.

"Oh, right."

Fiona walked through the dusting of new snow to the passenger side front door. She'd been getting strange vibes from Marc since he'd arrived. Would he be able to relax and be comfortable with her today?

"It's unlocked," he said, rounding the rear of the vehicle. He stopped. He was prepared for sledding, but not for whatever was going on between him and Fiona. He looked over the top of the vehicle at the tassel of her hat swaying behind her. Or was it only going on with him? Years of his mother and sisters drilling him on how to treat a woman kicked in. He should have opened the car door for Fiona, but it would be weird to walk back around and do it now.

He shook off the guilt. It wasn't as if they were on a

date. Fiona was Stella's aunt, like his sisters. He opened the back door for Stella. Except Fiona wasn't his sister. His gaze went to the front seat, to her face. The winter air had put a rosy flush on her cheeks. Her smiling lips were the same attractive tint. No, she wasn't his sister. Not by any stretch of the imagination. Stella pulled away from him to scramble into her car seat.

"Stella's seat. Daddy's seat. Feena's seat," she sang repeatedly as Marc, with one eye drawn to Fiona making herself comfortable in the front, fumbled with the fasteners on Stella's car seat. He wanted Stella to accept Fiona. That was the idea, but to accept her on her own, not as part of a package deal that included him.

"There you go," he said, after finally having to take his gloves off to snap the last fastener. He pulled his gloves back on, closed Stella's door and slid into the driver's seat.

"We're sledding at the golf course," he said as he backed onto Main Street. He shoved the car into Drive. She knew that. She'd gotten the same email from Noah that Marc had. "Have you ever been there?"

"No, I moved here in the fall after the course had closed for the season. Not that I've ever played."

"I could teach you in the spring." He gripped the steering wheel. Now what was he doing?

The corners of her mouth twitched. She was laughing at him. He couldn't blame her. "I think my skills lie more along the lines of miniature golf. It's something we could do with Stella."

Stella. He hadn't heard a peep out of her since she'd stopped singing. "Is she asleep?"

Fiona looked behind him. "Yep."

"That's good. She was up before six this morning raring to go. I should tell Mom a car ride is the key to getting Stella to nap. She's been giving her a hard time about it. I've been spending more time at the restaurant, and Mom has been watching her when she's not at school."

"Has the contractor run into more problems?"

"No, I've been getting myself and Stella into a routine of going into work every day, so it won't be a difficult transition when La Table Frais is up and running and I'll have to be there full time."

"I see."

Her casual comment struck him as almost judgmental. Why, he wasn't sure. But today he didn't seem to be sure about anything concerning Fiona.

"If you want to give your mother a break or spend a weekday with Stella, I could take her on a Saturday or Sunday so you could work—or evenings once you open."

He hadn't gotten as far as thinking about the evening hours. He should be more appreciative of Fiona's offer. Except Fiona seemed to be equating her spending time with Stella as the same as him spending time with his daughter.

"Sunday is family day. I haven't been working on Sundays." He could say that now, although that hadn't been the case with the restaurant downstate, and he couldn't guarantee he could completely avoid Sunday work here once La Table Frais opened.

A shadow crossed Fiona's face.

He had been depending on his mother for childcare a lot since he'd taken Fiona and Stella to see La Table Frais. Getting back to work had lifted some of the fog that had plagued him for so long and let him see a life where he was doing more than going through the motions, living for more than his daughter. It had made him realize he'd been ignoring God's message by turning into himself and not opening himself to His guidance for fulfilling the duties of a father.

"Stella might stay with you. She seemed comfortable with you today at your place." Even if he hadn't been. The apartment had seemed so full of Fiona, with pictures, knickknacks, books, bits of her life.

"Think about it," she said.

She and Stella were *all* he could think about.

"This should be fun," Fiona said, filling the silence. "I haven't been sledding in longer than I can remember."

Sledding, a nice neutral topic. "Me, either. It's the first winter Stella has been old enough. My wife wasn't much of an outdoor person."

Fiona slid him a sideways glance.

Why had he brought up Cate? He knew the answer. Old instincts. He wasn't proud of it, but he'd used the memory of Cate as a way to fend off any woman who'd expressed an interest in him. But Fiona's interest was in Stella. This time, he'd brought her up to fend off his own interest.

"Are you?" Fiona asked.

"Am I what?" Somehow he'd lost the thread of the conversation.

"An outdoor person?"

"Yes, I was, all seasons, although I haven't had much time the past few years. But I always tried to get in at least some skiing when we came up here for the holidays."

"I've always wanted to try skiing," Fiona said. "I've never been."

"I'm surprised," he said. "I mean, growing up around here. Didn't your high school have a ski team?" He bit his tongue. From what he'd gathered about Fiona's family, they probably couldn't have afforded the cost if she'd wanted to join a team.

"Yes, all of them did. I had to watch Mairi a lot, though, so Mom could work."

"I'm going to have to remedy that by taking you skiing. And Stella. I couldn't have been much older than she is the first time I went."

"Seriously, you started skiing when you were three?"

"About then. We all did. My mom skied competitively. She would have made the US national team if she hadn't broken her leg the week before final tryouts."

"Another reason I haven't tried skiing. I'm a chicken."

He jerked his head toward her. The admission surprised him. Everything he'd picked up about Fiona pointed to her being up for any challenge. "We'll start with the sledding, then, and see how it goes. Deal?"

Fiona grinned. "Deal."

"Here we are," he said a minute later, coming to a stop next to several other cars in the country club parking lot. "I'll wake up Stella."

"Want me to get the toboggan off the rack while you do?"

"If you want, you can undo the restraints. I'll get it down." He climbed out and opened the back door. "Stella, sweetpea." He touched her shoulder. "We're here at the hill to sled with your friends."

The little girl's eyes popped open and her gaze shot to the now-empty front seat. "Where's Feena? Feena friend."

"She's untying the toboggan."

"My saucer," Stella said as he unfastened her from her seat.

"It's in the back. We'll get it, too." He lifted Stella

out and walked her to the other side of the SUV, stopping to get Stella's snow saucer out on the way.

"All set," Fiona said.

He leaned the saucer against the SUV and lifted down the toboggan. "Who wants a ride?"

"Me, me." Stella hopped up and down before climbing on.

"I'd better grab your saucer," he said, holding the toboggan's pull rope in one hand and reaching for the other sled with the other.

"I can carry that," Fiona offered.

"Feena friend carry my saucer," Stella said.

Fiona's face brightened so that it outshone the afternoon sun on the sparkling snow. "I can do that."

"Teamwork. I like that," Marc said, passing the saucer to Fiona.

"Teamwork," Stella echoed.

Oblivious to the biting blast of wind that came off of Pharaoh Mountain, Marc walked with Fiona and Stella toward the low rectangular building where they were all meeting in the snack area. They could be a friendly team today.

This was more like it. Light, friendly. Fiona didn't know what caused Marc to seem so uncomfortable on the drive here. As for her, she was still basking in the glow of her niece calling her a friend, and she'd managed to keep her response low-key.

Fiona glanced sideways at Marc's strong profile and thought about his offer to take her skiing. While she wasn't sure she'd take him up on it, that was the sort of thing friends did. They were going to be seeing each other a lot while dealing with Stella, not to mention their work relationship. She could drop some of her reserve, let a friendship develop if it was going to. She'd kind of done that with Marc's twin, Claire, already.

When they reached the building, Stella hopped off the toboggan and Marc leaned it against a wall next to another sled.

"Stella," a high-pitched voice called from behind them.

A bundled-up little girl in a bright pink snowsuit plowed toward them at a pace that surprised Fiona.

"Daddy." Stella tugged on the bottom of his jacket as if he could have missed the child who was now right next to her. "Mia from school."

"Ah, your friend. Hi, Mia. And this is Ms.—"

"Fiona," she finished for him, remembering how Noah had called Marc's sister Ms. Renee at the balloon races.

"No." Stella stomped her little foot, making the light snow fly like a small white cloud. "No Ms. Fiona. Fiona friend."

Fiona would have picked Stella up and hugged her if she didn't know better than to push things.

"Hi, Fiona and Marc, isn't it?" Mia's aunt, whom Fiona had talked with at the adult meeting they'd gone to before the balloon races, caught up with her charge.

"Hi." Fiona wracked her brain for the woman's name and couldn't come up with it.

"Mia is all 'Stella this and Stella that' when I pick her up from The Kids Place after work on the days Stella comes. And there's a little boy, Luc, who apparently doesn't color up to the girls' standard."

Marc burst out laughing, softening the planes of his face and throwing off the underlying steel Fiona too often saw in his expression. "Poor Luc," he said. "The word is that he scribbles."

"Yes!" Stella said, followed by Mia's "outside the lines."

Mia's aunt slapped her mitten-covered hands to her cheeks. "Horrors," she said gaining another chuckle and a softer look from Marc.

The easy banter between Marc and Mia's aunt made Fiona wonder if they knew each other from school or something. That kind of back-and-forth had never come easy for Fiona, not with the flame of self-protection she'd always kept lit to guard her from blurting out something that, as her mother had always said, "people don't need to know about us."

"I'm sorry," Marc said. "I've forgotten your name."

"Katherine…Beagle. My friends call me Kat."

Fiona watched Marc struggle not to smile, disturbed by the kernel of want sprouting inside her for Marc to be as much at ease with her as he was with Kat.

"I know," Kat said. "I spent my early teen years dreaming of marriage just to get a different last name, but here I am, still Kat Beagle. Ruff."

Marc joined in Kat's laughter.

Fiona stepped closer to the two of them and tugged her hat down farther over her ears.

"It didn't help that I was taller than all of the boys, too thin and had braces and Coke-bottle glasses."

None of that described the vivacious brunette now. Fiona looked past Kat to the two little girls who'd walked closer to the building and the toboggans. Stella was pointing, and Mia touched one toboggan and then the other. The slight movement of one of the sleds caught Fiona's eye. She closed the few feet between her and the girls and grabbed both of them before the toboggans toppled down where the girls had been standing.

"Aunt Kat!" Mia tore away.

Fiona dropped to her knees and wrapped her arms around Stella. "It's okay." Her heart pounded.

"Too tight," Stella said, pushing at her.

Fiona let her go. Marc loomed above them, not saying anything. *Someone had to be watching them.* She sucked in her cheeks. Had she spoken aloud?

"She didn't scream," he said.

"Pardon?" A weight lifted from her shoulders. She hadn't spoken her criticism.

"Stella—she usually doesn't like people other than family touching her."

I am family. Fiona watched Marc disentangle the two toboggans.

The door to the clubhouse pushed opened. "Marc, Fiona, Kat, you're here," Noah said. "That makes everyone. Let's go." He motioned to the others keeping warm inside. They fanned out to retrieve their sledding equipment. "When we're done, we have cookies and hot chocolate and hot apple cider."

"Apples!" Stella repeated.

Marc frowned at the toboggan.

"Is there a problem?" Fiona asked.

"The food diary. Stella loves apples, but apples and nuts are foods that seem to bother her."

"The cider should be fine. It's the peels that are the problem. I noticed your mother used unpeeled apples in her apple crisp."

Marc wrinkled his forehead. Did he think she was criticizing his mother's baking? More than that, why was she being so hypersensitive?

"Stella loves Mom's apple crisp. It has walnuts, too. You checked out the websites Dr. Franklin gave us? I didn't," he admitted. "I thought I'd wait until after

Stella's next appointment when we know more. I didn't want to jump to conclusions."

Fiona tapped her boot in the snow. She knew Marc was concerned about Stella. Didn't he want to know as much as possible? Of course, Dr. Franklin hadn't made an actual diagnosis yet. "No, I knew from Beth."

His facial muscles tightened.

"Everyone ready?" Noah asked. "We're going to restrict our sledding to the longest gentle slope. Follow me."

"I'll grab Stella's saucer," Fiona said.

"No." Marc looked off into the distance. "We'd better stick to the toboggan. The crusty snow makes it too dangerous for the saucer."

Fiona didn't question him. Stella would be safer on the bigger sled, where Marc would have more control.

"Hop on, sweetpea,"

The little girl did, and the three of them followed the group.

When they reached the top of the hill, Noah pointed down. "My associate, Sara. Some of you met her in the clubhouse. She's at the bottom of the hill as our spotter." He waved and a woman in a plum-colored ski jacket waved back. "She'll signal 'all clear' for the next family, so we don't have any mishaps."

They lined up, with her, Marc and Stella near the end. But in no time, it was their turn.

"The snow looks fast," Marc said as he pulled the toboggan to the takeoff spot.

"Fast." Stella clapped.

After watching the other families zoom down, Fiona wasn't sure fast was good. She visualized the three of them loaded onto the toboggan, which seemed to have shrunk since he'd unloaded it from his SUV. She could sit in the front to steer and Stella could sit behind her as a buffer, with Marc in the back. Wouldn't that be safest?

"Me first," Stella said.

"That sounds good to me," Marc said. "You, Fiona and me. How does that sound to you, Fiona?"

Fiona restrained herself from asking, are you crazy? and pointed out what she thought was obvious. "Stella can't steer the toboggan."

Marc knit his brows. "Of course she can't. The ropes are long enough for me reach with my arms on either side of you and hold the lines to steer."

Yes, she could see that, and that was the problem. His arms enclosing her.

"You can hold on to Stella and put your feet on the curled front end to help me."

The satisfied expression on Marc's face said that he thought he had it all solved. Except his solution had her sandwiched between Stella and him. He lined up the toboggan and held it while Stella climbed on. Fiona followed, leaving Marc as much room behind her as she could.

"Take the ropes while I get on. I'll need my hands to push us off."

"Okay." She grabbed the ropes, wiggled a little closer to Stella and bent her knees closer into the little girl.

"Too tight," Stella said.

Fiona wriggled back. She couldn't risk one of the meltdowns Marc had told her about.

"Ready?" he asked.

Fiona breathed in the sharp winter air. "Yes." As ready as she was going to get.

Marc pushed off and took hold of the guide ropes, his strong arms still enclosing her.

"Whee!" Stella squealed with abandon.

Fiona relaxed in her little cocoon and enjoyed the ride.

Near the bottom of the hill, the toboggan hit a rock outcropping exposed by the earlier sledders. The impact bounced them into the air. Fiona felt every muscle in Marc's body stiffen as he yanked the ropes to keep them from turning over. He lost the battle, and Stella slipped out of Fiona's grasp. She and Marc tumbled after.

Pushing herself up to her knees from the face-plant she'd made in the snow, Fiona wiped the crusty flakes from her eyes and, heart pounding, searched out Stella. Marc already had her in his arms and was rubbing noses with his daughter and kissing her cheeks. Fiona allowed herself a moment to bask in the warmth of their family love.

"'Nuff kisses, Daddy. Down. Feena."

Marc placed Stella next to him and pivoted toward Fiona, a sheen of sweat on his cheeks.

Her shoulders dropped. He'd forgotten her. Fiona shook her head. What was she thinking? She couldn't expect him to be as concerned about her as he was about his daughter.

He placed her next to him. "You okay?" He offered Fiona a hand up.

"I'm fine." She let him draw her to her feet and brushed the snow off her jeans.

"You're sure?" He held onto her hand.

"I'm sure, but while Stella is probably good in her snowsuit, I'm afraid we may be feeling wet and cold in a few minutes."

"Kisses, Daddy."

Marc dropped Fiona's hand and reached to pick up Stella.

"Not me." Stella pushed at his hands.

Marc stilled. Then it hit Fiona. Stella had said *me*

instead of *Stella*. Fiona thought back to the other day when his eyes had lit and she couldn't read why... Stella had called Luc "my friend," not "Stella's friend." Her heart leaped at her niece's progress.

Stella pointed. Marc straightened and followed her little arm.

"Feena kisses."

Marc's gaze dropped to Fiona's lips. She unwillingly stepped forward at the same time he did, closing the distance between them to inches. She was no longer worried about feeling chilled. He leaned in. She mirrored his stance.

"Hey! You guys all right?" Sara, who'd been spotting at the bottom of the hill, reached them.

Fiona jumped back.

"Yes," Marc answered, the word a combination of strangled and gruff.

"More," Stella said, grabbing her father's hand and tugging him toward the overturned toboggan.

"I need to get a little warm and dry before I take another run," she said. *If I take another run.*

Sara made an okay sign up the hill, and Fiona started the trek up.

She touched her gloved fingers to her lips and shivered. Marc had wanted to kiss her. Right in front of everyone on the hill. And she hadn't wanted to stop him.

Chapter Nine

He'd become a coward. Since last weekend's sledding trip with the Bridges group, Marc couldn't get the vision of Fiona's upturned face, rosy cheeks and lips and Stella chanting "kisses" out of his head. He couldn't deny it. He had wanted to kiss Fiona and had a gut feeling she hadn't been against the idea. He'd thrown himself into his work, just as he had in New York when life had gotten hard for him. He slammed his SUV to a stop in his parents' driveway behind Fiona's car.

What was she doing here? Tracking him down for his evasive responses to the couple texts she'd sent him? In his dreams. Both of the texts had been about work. He trudged to the kitchen door, let himself in and stomped off the snow—and some of his agitation—on the mat just inside.

His mother's voice floated through from the dining room. "I really thought he'd be here by now, before Stella fell asleep."

He had, too. Stella rarely fell asleep for anyone but him. But he'd gotten involved in the hands-on work of laying the tile for the kitchen floor, and then one of the guys had had to leave. Marc had volunteered to stay. The physical labor had felt good.

"She curled right up and nodded off on the couch before I finished reading her the story she wanted," Fiona said.

Mom laughed. "Yeah, with John's TV program and snoring providing the right amount of monotonous background noise to keep her asleep."

"I should head out," Fiona said.

He heard the slide of a chair on the hardwood floor as he approached the dining room doorway.

"Thanks for dinner."

Fiona had come for dinner? How had he missed that?

"Thank you for your ideas."

Ideas. What was his mother cooking up?

"Stay a minute and let me tell you about Stella's doctor's appointment today. I had hoped to tell you and Marc together."

That was another act of cowardice, taking his mother up on her offer to take Stella to her follow-up with Dr. Franklin. He'd convinced himself she could handle it better than him, just as Cate always had.

"You can tell us together." Marc walked into the dining room and pulled out the chair next to Fiona.

"Hi." She smiled at him, needling his heart.

"Hey."

"We missed you at dinner," his mother said, glancing at Fiona.

Fiona tugged at her shirtsleeve. "We got together with Claire, Andie and Natalie to plan Renee's baby shower."

"Right." Marc vaguely remembered his mother saying something about that, but not about Fiona coming to dinner. Wasn't that what he wanted? His family to treat Fiona as one of them, for Fiona to spend time with Stella without him? Then why were his mother's and Fiona's words making him feel guilty about the extra work hours he'd put in lately?

"So what did Dr. Franklin say?" Marc held his breath waiting for his mother's response.

"The tests point to some type of IBD."

"Inflammatory bowel disease," Fiona said.

"I know that." His words came out sharper than he meant them to, but the results weren't what he'd wanted to hear, even if they were what he'd expected deep down.

"Dr. Franklin did another test today," his mother continued, "and set up an appointment for an ultrasound. I know you're busy. Fiona said she could take Stella. I have a dentist appointment at the same time."

"I can take her." He sensed rather than saw Fiona tense beside him. "Fiona and I can." He shouldn't let his mixed feelings toward Fiona interfere with her relationship with Stella and his family. Who was he to say who they could be friends with?

His mother folded her hands on the table. "Good. The appointment is two weeks from Thursday at ten. I'll give you the reminder card."

Earlier today, he'd made plans to meet with the linen supplier that morning to finalize selections and delivery. "No problem." Maybe he could switch it to later in the day and take Stella with him. He shook his head. After putting her through an ultrasound, he and Stella should do something fun. Invite Fiona to come with them, if she could take the whole day off.

"Something wrong with that date?" Fiona asked. "You shook your head."

"It was something else. Unrelated."

Fiona's eyes narrowed, and he looked away.

"Dr. Franklin and I went over Stella's food journal, and I shared it with Fiona. Do you two want to talk about that here or in the front room?" his mother asked. "I have a TV show I want to catch. You'd be more comfortable in the front room. Your father has a nice fire going in there."

Marc rubbed his leg. As if he'd be more comfortable anywhere, alone with Fiona.

"Go on." His mother handed him the food journal and made a shooing motion. "And Fiona, thanks again for the suggestion for my apple crisp. I'll do that next time I make it."

That would be a first—his mother taking a suggestion for one of her signature desserts.

"What did you say to my mother about her apple crisp?" he asked as they walked through the dining room.

"The same as I mentioned to you, that the apple peels and nuts were most likely what had bothered Stella, not the sugar, as your mother thought."

"Mom didn't say anything to me."

"That was before she'd talked with Dr. Franklin."

At the appointment he should have taken his daughter to. He stopped beside the couch where Stella lay fast asleep, struck by how much she looked like her aunt. Fiona could easily be taken as Stella's mother. Dr. Franklin had thought so.

Marc fisted his left hand, the one blocked from Fiona's view. Cate had been Stella's mother. He was Stella's father. All Fiona wanted to be was Stella's aunt, which was why he had to get their almost-kiss on the hill out of his mind. He bent and kissed Stella's forehead. That was the only kissing he should be thinking about.

He straightened, taking care not to accidentally brush Fiona, who stood right behind him. "The front room is off to the right."

She fell into step with him.

"Now, what were you saying about Dr. Franklin?" The warmth emanating from the woodstove hit him before they entered the front room.

"He and your mother hit it off."

"That's good. I had concerns about Mom taking things seriously."

Fiona shot him a questioning look he couldn't read. But, despite his four sisters, when had he ever been able to read women? He took in the room. Mom's ancient cat, Kiddles, was asleep on the chair he was going to sit in. That left only the love seat. For the two of them. Mentally fortifying himself, he motioned to the love seat and sat next to Fiona, as far away as the overstuffed cushions would allow.

"I think she is now, at least," Fiona said. "She took notes. They're at the back of the journal."

Marc flipped the journal open. He was glad his mother was acknowledging Stella might have a medical condition, but he hoped, now that Mom had, she didn't jump in with two feet and blow it out of proportion as she sometimes did.

"I didn't know you were coming to dinner tonight." He couldn't remember his mother mentioning anything about that when he'd dropped Stella off this morning.

"She called to check whether I was coming this evening for the planning session and invited me. She said Stella was here."

His mother had Fiona's phone number? "Right. Renee's baby shower." Marc read through his mother's notes from the doctor's appointment.

"Stella seems to be sensitive to many of the same foods Beth was," Fiona said when he finished.

"But Dr. Franklin hasn't diagnosed Stella with Crohn's."

Fiona avoided his gaze. "No, he hasn't."

"The ultrasound and other tests could rule it out."

"They could."

Marc placed the journal on the arm of the love seat and dropped his head into his hands. "How did your mother do it? Your sister was little, like Stella."

Fiona stiffened. "She didn't." The flatness of her voice didn't hide all the anger that radiated from Fiona. "I did the best I could to help."

His heart somersaulted. "You were a child, too."

"I listened at the doctors' appointments and read the information they gave my mother so I could remind her not to buy foods that were bad for Beth."

"Where was your father?"

"He didn't accept Beth's diagnosis or treatment, and then he left."

As he hadn't fully accepted his wife's diagnosis or fully appreciated his family's closeness and support.

He took Fiona's hand in his, and she squeezed it. At that moment, he wanted nothing in the world more than to protect Fiona every bit as much as he wanted to protect and take care of his daughter.

She had to get out of here. The cozy room, complete with crackling fire. Marc's nearness, his hand wrapped around hers. His mother, his sisters, the whole big family. It had her wanting things that weren't hers to want, like a place in Marc's life beyond simply being Stella's aunt. But she made no attempt to move, wanting to bask in the warm bubble of security she felt for the moment—security she knew couldn't last, not for her. The only security she could depend on was what she provided herself.

"Stella seems to be warming to you, letting you read her a story tonight and sledding with her on Saturday."

The room hung thick with the unsaid words: *when we almost kissed.*

Fiona untangled her hand. "I should go. Work tomorrow."

Her gaze followed Marc's to the grandfather clock in the corner of the room. Seven fifteen. Not exactly the dead of the night.

"Stay."

Her heart tripped.

"We should talk about Stella."

Stella, right. What had she been thinking?

He crossed his ankle over his other leg, knee toward her. "If Stella has something more, IBS or Crohn's disease, like your sister did…you'll help me?"

Fiona knew Marc well enough to know how difficult him asking her for help was.

"With everything I have," she said.

His hopeful expression darkened. What had she said wrong?

"I didn't handle my wife's illness well."

"I can only imagine how difficult it was."

"It was, especially with Stella not really understanding what was going on." He jiggled his knee. "But that's not what I mean. I've accepted God's will. What I haven't done is forgiven myself for some of my actions the last few months of Cate's life." His voice broke. "I wouldn't accept it was fatal, not even after she had."

"There's nothing wrong with hope."

He stopped bouncing his knee. "Sometimes there is."

She flinched. Stella wasn't his late wife. She wasn't

Beth. From what Dr. Franklin had told them and Marc's mother, anything the doctor suspected would be treatable. Not knowing what to say, Fiona waited for Marc to continue, evidently unable to disguise what she was feeling.

"I don't mean Stella," he reassured her, taking Fiona's hand in his again.

If he was looking for strength, she'd give him all she had. Fiona looked into his troubled eyes. And not only for Stella's sake.

"Toward the end, Cate was in intense pain. She was ready to leave us, and I couldn't bear that. I pushed her and her oncologist to try everything and threw myself into work, fooling myself that I was doing it for her, to pay for experimental treatments our insurance didn't cover." He dropped his head to his chin. "I was doing it for myself, and I harmed the two people I loved most."

For a selfish moment, Fiona wondered what it would be like to have the kind of love she could see Marc had had for his late wife, and that he had for Stella.

"We can work together to manage Stella's condition without taking away her joy."

"You think so? I changed my mind and read the information on the websites Dr. Franklin gave us. Some possible triggers are Stella's favorite foods, like Mom's apple crisp."

"Which is why I suggested to her that she try making it with peeled apples and not nuts. I'm sure Stella will still like it. It's just being vigilant with small things like that."

Marc uncrossed his legs and stretched them toward the fire. "Stella regressed behavior-wise under my care after Cate…" He didn't finish.

"You discussed that with her doctor?"

"Of course I did."

Fiona pressed back into the soft cushion of the love seat at the vehemence of his words. Marc, his family—they weren't her family.

"And I took her to a counselor downstate and talked over the situation with Renee."

"I'm sorry. You and your family aren't like my family."

The edge left his expression. He squeezed her hand, and joy bubbled through her.

"The two things that worried me most about Stella's behavior since Cate's death," he stumbled a bit over the last word, "are her fear, even anger, toward women Cate's age who might remind her of Cate, and her delayed speech."

"Stella's been hesitant with me, but I haven't seen what I'd call true anger toward me."

Marc looked thoughtfully at the fire. "You're right." He told her about a few of the heartbreaking outbursts he'd seen from Stella.

Could the little girl sense they were related? Fiona quickly quashed that idea. "She may have accepted me because you and Noah introduced me as your and Claire's friend."

A slow smile spread across Marc's face. Fiona let herself believe a tiny part of that smile might be for her.

"Could be. And I don't know if you've noticed, but Stella has been increasingly using 'me' and 'I' and 'my' when referring to herself, rather than 'Stella.'"

Marc's words confirmed the thoughts Fiona had had about the funny looks she'd seen on his face when they'd been with Stella. "I'm certainly no expert, but I think your time off work with Stella has made her feel more secure."

"The question is, secure enough for me to be back at work? I'm beginning to be jazzed about the restaurant opening, finding the satisfaction I'd always had in my work again."

Fiona fought the hollow opening in her stomach. Would she be able to fill the gap with Stella if Marc became overly absorbed in his work, as it sounded like he'd been before his wife's death? She didn't want that responsibility, the possibility of failing again.

"Your sister or Noah would be better able to answer that." She took a deep breath. "But I want to be clear that I'd have trouble standing by quietly and watching you put work before Stella."

Marc's glacial stare dropped the temperature in the air between them by twenty degrees. "You think I would do that?"

"Not intentionally."

He sucked in a breath. "I did do that. Cate picked up the slack."

"As much as I'm growing to love Stella, I can't do that for you."

"I'd never ask you to do all of what Cate did for Stella, any more than I'd ask one of my sisters to. Cate was her mother."

Although they shouldn't have, his words seemed framed to keep Fiona in her place. She buried her hurt and composed herself. "And, like your sisters, I'm her aunt. What I can do is tell you if I think you're neglecting Stella."

Marc drew back at the word *neglect*.

"That was a little strong. Getting off balance is what I meant," Fiona clarified.

"I knew what you meant. I may have neglected Stella at times in an emotional sense, knowing Cate was there for me, and after when I was drowning in grief and re-sponsibility."

Fiona squeezed his hand and he favored her with a smile, the smile she often caught on his face when he was looking at Stella. Her heart thumped.

"So what you said about keeping me on the straight and narrow where work and Stella are concerned? It's a deal."

The fire popped and crackled as the top log split and fell to the floor of the stove. She had exactly what she wanted, her place as Stella's aunt. So why was the hollow feeling in her stomach still there?

"Has Fiona gone home?" His mother caught him standing beside the couch where Stella was still fast asleep. Only his dad had been in the living room watching TV when he'd walked Fiona to the door.

"Yes, just now. Did you need her for something?"

His mother shook her head. "No, but do you have a minute?"

"I should get Stella home." He knew that argument was useless, but tried anyway. He didn't want his mother bursting the bubble of warmth he still felt from the conversation he'd shared with Fiona.

"She can sleep here as well as at your house. Come into the kitchen where we won't disturb your father."

He followed her and sat at the table, purposely looking at the clock above the sink.

"This won't take long," his mother said.

"It's about Fiona?" He braced himself.

"Yes, I like her."

That certainly wasn't what he expected. "I do, too," he blurted.

His mother smiled.

"Not like that," he protested.

"Like what?"

He ignored her question. "I knew you were okay with her after our lunch. You didn't need to reassure me."

"I did. Spending time with her tonight, seeing her with your sisters and especially with Stella, let me get to know Fiona better. I really like her."

Marc shifted in his seat. "I'm glad. Is that it?"

"Not so fast. Did you have a good talk?"

He had no idea what was going on with his mother. This was reminiscent of her cornering him on his way in the house after his first real date, the homecoming dance his sophomore year in high school—and his first kiss. His thoughts drifted to holding Fiona on the country club hill, her eyes wide with surprise when he'd leaned in.

Marc cleared his throat. "We did. Her knowledge and experience with her sister, even if Fiona was a child herself, will be helpful." He sounded so clinical, but how else should he sound with his mother? He couldn't show how warm and jumbled he really felt.

"That's all?"

Pretty much all he wanted to share. "Fiona said she'd step up and tell me if I'm veering toward becoming a workaholic again."

"Good. That's what got you in trouble before, burying yourself in work so you couldn't see anything else."

Stick it to me, Mom. "It was more complicated than that, but I get your gist."

"Working with you and your partners should help her see how much you're working and help manage that."

He didn't need his mother or Fiona managing him. Marc leaned back on the rear legs of his chair, earning him a glare from his mother. He dropped the chair to the floor. Although his mother's grilling had him feeling like an adolescent, he didn't need to act like one.

"Fiona was very good stepping in for you tonight with Stella when you had to work so late."

"Yes, I thanked her. Frankly, I was surprised. You know how Stella can be around strange women."

"Stella doesn't see her as a stranger anymore, now that you two have been spending more time with her."

"Spending time with Fiona as Stella's aunt," he felt compelled to clarify for his mother and, admittedly, a bit for himself.

"Stella was all about Fiona this, Fiona's house that this afternoon. I hadn't realized the three of you had spent time there." His mother smiled.

"We stopped by to pick up Fiona for the Bridges sledding party."

"Stella told me all about the party, too."

His face flushed. No way could Stella have known he'd been about to kiss Fiona. "We had a lot of fun."

"She also said something about watching her *Frozen* movie at Fiona's, and you cooking."

"We talked about that. Fiona offered to take Stella on a Saturday if I needed to work." He ignored the look his mother gave him about working on a Saturday. "While Stella was fine at Fiona's when we were there, I'm not sure how comfortable she'd be if I wasn't with her, so I said we could all do it sometime. I'd make lunch."

"Then you won't mind that I invited Fiona to join us at the End of Winter Celebration in Ticonderoga?"

Marc scratched his head. How had Mom gone from Stella watching a movie with Fiona to the End of Winter Celebration?

"Fiona said that although she'd lived in Ticonderoga as a child, she's never been."

If his mother had the few glimpses he'd had into Fiona's childhood, she wouldn't find that at all strange.

"The whole family is going," she went on.

"What did Fiona say?" It would be fun taking Fiona.

"She said she'd get back to me. I told her to go ahead and get back to you."

Marc closed his eyes and counted to three. "Do you remember what happened the last time you tried to fix me up with someone?" He faked a shudder.

"I've never done that. Besides, this is a family tradition. Fiona is family now."

Right. They were all family. But he doubted he and his mother and Fiona were on the same page, or even in the same book, on the definition of his and Fiona's family relationship. Maybe it was time he did something about clarifying that.

Chapter Ten

Fiona fussed with the curly streamers of ribbon she'd made on top of Stella's wrapped birthday gift. She hoped the little girl would like the Elsa doll castle she'd bought her. When she'd gotten back to Marc about coming to the End of Winter Celebration with him and his family today, she'd asked him what Stella might like for her birthday. He'd seemed nearly as clueless as her but said she couldn't go wrong with anything from *Frozen* and rattled off what Stella already had.

Pulling one of the streamers out and letting it pop back, Fiona remembered the talking family dollhouse her parents had gotten her and Mairi for Christmas the year the mill where her stepfather had worked closed. Fiona wondered now if they had used his severance pay for gifts that year. It was the most lavish Christmas she remembered.

Her eyes prickled with unshed tears. How she and Mairi had loved that dollhouse. They'd still dragged it out and played with it when they were far older than the ages it was meant for. That's why she grabbed the castle when she saw it on the shelf.

Fiona put Stella's gift in the bag from the store to protect it from the light snow falling and bounded down the stairs to her car. Tossing the gift on the passenger's seat, she put her key in the ignition and turned. All she got was a clicking noise. She tried again and got the same.

Fiona slapped the steering wheel before she whipped out her phone. Hopefully, Marc hadn't already left and wouldn't mind picking her up. He shouldn't since he'd already offered. She'd been the one who'd insisted on driving herself, in case she hit a point where she felt uncomfortable surrounded by his family—or with him and the growing feelings she might have trouble hiding.

"Hey," she said when he answered his phone. "Does that ride offer still stand?"

"Sure."

"My car won't start," she added, by way of explanation.

"You caught us just in time. We were headed for the door."

"Okay, then I'll expect you in a few minutes."

"We'll be there."

Had she caught an upbeat tone in his voice, or was it only that she wanted to hear one? Same as last week, she'd only spoken with Marc a couple of times this week. Both times he'd sounded harried and had said he was busy trying to get everything to come together with the restaurant setup. Most likely, any difference she'd heard in his voice today had been because he was glad for the weekend and some downtime with Stella—as if there was any downtime with an active three-year-old.

Fiona called Hill's Garage about her car and ran a set of keys over to Mrs. Hamilton to give to the tow truck driver when he arrived. Then she waited outside for Marc and Stella. "Happy birthday, birthday girl," she said over the seat back as she slid into Marc's SUV.

"I'm free now," Stella said, holding up her mitten-clad hand with what Fiona assumed was three fingers raised.

"I know you are. You're getting to be such a big girl." Fiona's mind flitted to Beth, who hadn't been much older than Stella when she'd died.

Stella beamed with a smile so like Mairi's that it sent a shot of happy nostalgia through Fiona, lifting the pallor of her other memory.

"Feena come to my party?"

Fiona looked over at Marc. He hadn't said anything about a party. Nor had his mother. The party must be tomorrow, since the carnival lasted until after dark today if they stayed for the fireworks. Fiona repositioned the bag with Stella's gift on the car floor. Of course, she couldn't expect to be invited to every Delacroix family event, but to be left out of Stella's birthday was a blow. She shook off an all-too-familiar feeling of exclusion.

"Stella thinks the carnival is her birthday party, no matter what any of us have told her," Marc explained.

Fiona's heart lifted. "Works for me. It's her birthday, and there's food and games. Sounds like a party to me." She winked at Stella, who blinked back with a giggle.

"And to warn you." Marc shifted in his seat. "Mom is playing along with Stella. She plans to buy a cake at the bake sale, put in candles and sing right before the fireworks start. She's sure we'll have no trouble getting a couple of tables to have the cake in the Armory where the refreshment stands are."

"What, no ice cream?"

"Don't even mention it, or she'll send someone in search of some."

Fiona laughed, egging him on. "We can do it large

and have her open gifts, too." Fiona lifted the bag she'd brought from the floor.

"You've been hanging out with my mother too much."

His laugh rumbled through her. *And not as much as I'd like to with you,* the voice in the back of her head said. "I'd really like to see her open my gift." Fiona couldn't keep the joyful anticipation of having found what she thought was the perfect gift out of her voice— or her heart.

"That must be some present."

"I hope so." She should be more careful not to set herself up for disappointment in case Stella wasn't as enthused.

He shook his head. "You're as bad as Mom. What am I going to do with you?"

Once again her internal voice intruded. *Love me,* it shouted, silently assuming the little-girl persona Fiona had thought she'd permanently shed. What was it about Marc that stripped her down to her bare essence?

"Birthday present?" Stella asked, leaning forward in her car seat, trying to see the bag Fiona held.

"Shh." Fiona pressed her fingers to her lips. "Not until after we have cake. First, we have to see the clown, have our faces painted, try out the bouncy house and get a balloon animal." She rattled off the carnival activities she'd read about in the newspaper that she thought Stella would like.

"Balloons." Stella clapped.

"And," Marc said, "ice skate and try a round of miniature golf. At the Bridges sledding party when I said I'd teach you to golf, you said miniature golf was more your speed."

"Don't you think Stella is too little for skating and golf?"

"Yes, I meant you and me. I have the twins lined up as a relief team so we can spend some time together."

Fiona fingered the handle of the plastic bag. "Your nieces? Are you sure Stella will be okay with them?"

"Stella's fine with them, and you had to have noticed that she's becoming less timid with other women overall."

Fiona avoided his gaze. She knew Stella was more comfortable around her. Was Marc lumping her in with the crowd? She swallowed the lump building in her throat. After their almost-kiss while sledding with Stella and the cozy talk in front of the wood fire—not to mention his mother's one-eighty pivot to considering Fiona one of the family—Fiona had found it difficult to block thoughts that maybe their relationship could be about more than Stella.

"I wouldn't exactly call your nieces women," she managed.

Marc creased his brow. She hadn't meant to sound so strident. A lot of people used teenage babysitters. But Stella was special—and she needed special care.

"They're seventeen going on eighteen. You couldn't have been much older when you had custody of Mairi."

"I was a college sophomore." He was right about not being much older in years, but she had been in responsibility and experience. "And there'll be a lot of people there. Strangers."

"She'll be fine. You worry too much. I'll ask Mom to keep an eye on all of them."

Fiona bit her lip. She wasn't faulting Terry Delacroix. Maybe it was because she'd raised six kids, including two sets of twins, but Marc's mother was pretty casual with her grandchildren. Certainly nothing like the way her own mother had been, but...

"Hey, you okay?" Marc reached over and squeezed her shoulder.

She had to brace herself not to give away the shiver that his touch sent through her despite the heated seat and warm air blasting from the dashboard.

"It'll give you and me some time together. I've been so busy with work that we've hardly talked the past two weeks."

"I'd like that." A smile spread across her face. Fiona relaxed back into her seat. *Time together.* She did like the sound of that, even if she might be reading too much into it. It was Stella's birthday. She was spending it with the little girl for the first time, with food and games and companionship.

Her glance slid sideways to Marc, taking in his broad shoulders, running down his arms that she didn't need to see beneath his coat to know their power and sense the inner strength he exuded. Despite any inclination he might have to get caught up in his work and momentarily put it ahead of family, that inner strength told her that he was a man who would fight tooth and nail for his family and other loved ones if challenged.

Marc caught her appraising him, and the right corner of his mouth quirked up.

Fiona willed her cheeks not to flush and pointed out the windshield to his left. "Was that an eagle?" she asked.

"I must have missed it," he said. "I was looking at the scenery to my right."

She lost out to the flush and looked out the passenger window. While gathering her scattered emotions and putting them back in their safe compartments, an uncharacteristic thought struck her. Why not release them and see where they went? Today might be the perfect time to apply the letting-go techniques of the online Christian meditation Noah was doing with her and some of the others in the adult Bridges group.

Relax and let whatever would be happen. No stops. No regrets.

"Party!" Stella shouted minutes later when they arrived at the Armory in Ticonderoga.

"Yes, we're at the carnival." Marc helped her out of the SUV, knowing she didn't catch his correction. But he needed to tamp down her excitement some, or they could be in for a long day. Then again, what did it matter if they let Stella think the festivities were for her birthday? He didn't think she had that firm a grasp on what a birthday party was to have many expectations. Her only reference was the little party her group had had at The Kids Place for her friend Mia's birthday. This would serve fine as Stella's party.

His lungs burned. His mother had planned a party last winter for Stella's second birthday, and they were going to come up. But there had been some last-minute personnel problems at the restaurant and he'd felt he had to stay and cover. Stella's usual babysitter hadn't been available on the short notice, so he'd had to use a childcare service. His baby had spent her birthday with a stranger.

Looking back, he saw he could have gotten coverage for the restaurant. What it came down to was that after the agony of having spent Christmas at his folks' without Cate, he hadn't been ready to face his big rambunctious family again only a couple months later. Lord help him, but he'd welcomed the excuse not to come celebrate Stella's birthday in Paradox Lake last year.

"Daddy! Let's go." Stella tugged his hand.

"All right. Let me get your backpack and lock the car."

He watched Fiona walk around the front of the vehicle while he grabbed Stella's things. His heart turned over. From the bounce in her step, Fiona might be as excited about the carnival as Stella was. She'd said she'd never been before, and for whatever reason, he liked the feeling that he was the one introducing her to this local and family tradition.

"Do you have everything you need, Fiona? Before I lock the car."

"I do," she said in a bright voice that matched her step. "I'm going to leave the you-know-what in the car and get it later when we're ready to have cake."

"Birthday cake," Stella said. "With fire, Gammy said."

"You mean with candles." Fiona joined them. "Three because you're three today."

"Free! Fire!"

Marc caught Fiona's gaze as he shook his head. He laughed. "We'd better watch it. I think we may be raising a little pyromaniac here."

The smile Fiona gave him in return outshone the bright winter sun on the pristine layer of new snow that had covered the ground while they were driving here. He suddenly felt overdressed despite the bite to the air.

They were doing that, he realized, raising Stella together—as much or more than he and Cate had, since he was much more active and responsible a father now. His heart ached for what he and Cate had and hadn't had, but that was in the past. As for Fiona's contention that she wanted nothing more than to be Stella's aunt, she did far more for Stella than his sisters did. Not that he'd asked much of them lately, or nearly as much of his mother. He seemed to naturally think of Fiona first, and not only when he needed help with Stella.

"Daddy, you're a slowpoke."

He dragged his gaze from Fiona. "I didn't know we're in that much of a hurry."

"We don't want to miss anything, do we, Stella?" Fiona asked.

"No." Stella shook her head so hard, the ties of her snowsuit hood came loose.

Marc released Stella's hand and bent to tie the strings.

"Hold hand," Stella ordered when he righted himself.

Marc slipped his hand around his daughter's.

"Feena, too," she said. "No get lost."

"We talked about the crowds and sticking close so neither one of us gets lost," he explained.

Fiona moved to the other side of Stella and reached for her hand.

"No, Daddy's hand. He's big and strong."

The corners of Fiona's mouth twitched as she readily moved to his other side and slipped her hand into his with no hesitation.

Marc braced for a repeat of the jolt of attraction he'd felt when he'd squeezed her shoulder in the car. His gaze dropped to her at his side. From her lack of a discernable reaction at either touch, she must not have felt anything. He scuffed the toe of his boot in the snow. Fiona had made it abundantly clear that all she wanted was to be Stella's aunt. That's where their relationship ended.

She shivered.

Or did his touch affect her after all?

"Let's go inside," she said. "I'm getting cold out here."

Cold? His temperature had risen a couple more degrees. So much for his touch affecting her like hers did him.

He cleared the scratch from his throat as the three of them started toward the building. "Mom said for us to all meet by the photo booth." Which now had him wondering if Mom had plans for them other than simply meeting there. Fiona might like a picture of her and Stella. Or they could have one taken of the three of them. As a remembrance of Stella's birthday, not because he wanted a picture of Fiona. He had enough virtual ones plaguing him at inopportune times.

"That's the info she gave me, too, not that I have any idea where the photo booth might be."

"Mom called you to check on us? To see whether you were coming?"

"No, she called about Renee's baby shower and asked if I had the agenda for today."

He hadn't realized there was an agenda, except for the cake later and his plan to carve out some time alone with Fiona.

"When I said I was driving myself, she checked to make sure I knew where to find everyone."

"Good, I wanted to make sure Mom wasn't up to anything." *Like pushing me at you.* He wanted to take that journey at his own pace.

Fiona laughed.

"You don't know my mother. One time…" He started to tell her about one of her matchmaking escapades and stopped. Showing Fiona his dorky high-school self wasn't any way to impress her. Was that what he wanted to do? He tightened his hold on her hand. Yeah, maybe it was.

"Over here," his mother called when they got within thirty feet of the photo booth. "Since everyone is here now, I want the photographer to get a family photo before everyone goes off in their own direction."

Marc groaned, and Fiona elbowed him.

"I think it's nice."

"You've never sat for a Delacroix family photo session," he said.

"Hi, Fiona," his mother said when they joined the group. "And here's my birthday girl." She gave both of them a hug.

"I'm ready for you, Mrs. Delacroix," the photographer said. "And Marc, is it?"

Mom had never met anyone she didn't immediately consider a friend. Except Fiona, and she'd more than made up for that since their rocky beginning.

"I'd like you in the center back with Pastor Connor, Paul and Rhys." The guys took their places. "Now your sisters and Fiona in front of you."

"No," Fiona demurred. "It's a family picture. I'll have one of Stella and me taken afterward."

"That's fine," his mother said, "but you're family, and I'd like you in this one."

"I would, too." Marc kept his voice low, for Fiona's ears only.

"But what if—" she started to protest.

"There are no *if*s. You're family."

Fiona's face went soft and dewy, making his heart swell with longing. *His family.* If he didn't mess it up.

The photographer finished.

"Now, I'd like one of each of you and your families alone," his mother said.

Marc wasn't the only one who groaned this time, but

they all obliged. Marc and Fiona and Stella went last, with Fiona hesitating again.

"Go ahead," Paul said. "If my lummox of an older brother botches things later, I can Photoshop him out, and you'll have a nice portrait of you and Stella."

Marc fisted and released his hands. *No.* He wasn't going to mess anything up. He'd learned his lesson with Cate and Stella. Besides, there was nothing concrete between him and Fiona to ruin—yet. He took his place next to Fiona, whom the photographer had already positioned with Stella on her lap.

"Put your arm around Fiona," the photographer said.

Marc held his breath and slid his arm along the back of the chair behind Fiona. There was no spark this time, but rather a very right feeling that spoke of a possibility of a new beginning. He drank in the beauty beside him, seeing so many of Fiona's features in Stella. Anyone who didn't know them could take Fiona for Stella's mother.

He tucked that piece of information into his heart. There was no way he was going to mess this up.

Chapter Eleven

"Ha!" Several hours later, Fiona aced the last hole of the miniature golf course set up in the Armory at two under par. She leaned on her golf club, blew on her fingernails and rubbed them on her shirt.

"Are we a little full of ourselves?" Marc asked, completing the hole in three shots.

"Not at all. That puts me two points ahead for the game." She scrutinized his grinning face. "You didn't let me win, did you?"

He raised his hands in mock surrender. "Excuse me? I grew up in a household with four sisters. I know the power of women. I don't *let* them do anything. I simply try to hold my own. And it isn't easy."

"Poor guy. I feel for you."

"To be serious. You've got good form…uh, golfing form."

"I knew what you meant." That was one of the many things she liked about Marc. He was always straight with her. None of the hidden meanings she'd grown up with in her family. She checked the time on her phone. "Looks like we're going to have to bag the ice-skating."

"You don't sound disappointed," Marc said.

She was and she wasn't. Gliding around the outdoor rink, Marc's arm around her waist to guide her, had real appeal. A more likely reality would be Marc pulling her up repeatedly from a heap on the ice.

"I am a little, but I had a lot of fun spending the time with Stella, getting our faces painted and watching her in the bouncy house. And with Luc and the twins trying the Wii Dance Dance Revolution."

"She and Luc were a riot."

"Can I admit something to you?"

"You can admit anything you want."

"I kind of liked that Stella didn't want to go with the twins, that she wanted to stay with us."

"Me, too." Marc's eyes darkened in a way that did funny things to her heart. "Even though it cut down on our time together."

"All right, guys." Claire appeared out of nowhere. "If you two are through making goo-goo eyes at each other, why don't you turn your equipment in and join the rest of us for supper?"

"Do I detect a hint of jealousy?" Marc made a show of looking around, as if trying to find someone.

"Back off," Claire said. "Nick is here talking with Dad and Paul."

Fiona's knees wobbled at the teasing. She steeled them with reality. His words were simply lighthearted family dynamics. Weren't they? Or had her instincts about Marc's interest in her been right? She so rarely acknowledged her instincts that she wasn't sure.

"I need to get Stella's birthday gift from the car," Fiona said. "I want to see her open it."

Claire nodded. "Give Marc your keys. He can get it and meet us over by the picnic tables."

"It's in my car anyway," he said. "Fiona came with me."

"I see," Claire said knowingly.

"I'll be back in a couple minutes." Marc strode off, leaving Fiona to flush.

"I was sure Mom had said you were driving yourself."

Marc's mother and sisters talked about them? This was one part of being a member of a large family that wasn't so warm and fuzzy.

"My car wouldn't start. I caught Marc as he and Stella were leaving."

"Uh-huh."

"So, Nick?" Fiona deflected Claire's comment. "As in Nick who we work with?"

"Yeah, we're kind of on-again, off-again. More friends than anything else. Mom saw him and invited him to eat with us. But we're not talking about me and Nick. We're talking about you and my little brother."

"Little brother?" Fiona pictured Marc as he'd been a minute ago, standing next to Claire and towering over her.

"Younger brother by ten minutes, and I never let him forget it. Moving on—he's got it bad for you."

"We're just friends, like you and Nick."

"I don't think so. Since you came into his life, he's been more alive than I've seen him in a good long time, since before Cate got sick."

"Grieving takes time, has stages. It's different for everyone." Fiona paraphrased what the family court counselor had told them when they'd seen her following their mother's death during the custody proceedings.

"You do have feelings for him, beyond him being Stella's father?"

This kind of question usually raised her shield

against sharing her personal family business. Except Claire was family. Fiona gulped a breath. "I do."

"Does he know?"

"I haven't told him in so many words."

"Then he doesn't know," Claire stated. "Tell him. When it comes to personal things, he's not as confident as he appears. But promise me one thing. If you're not serious, let him know that, too. Don't hurt him."

Don't hurt *him*? "I won't. Not intentionally." She had too much to lose, including Claire's friendship, she suspected. Fiona couldn't remember the last close girlfriend she'd had besides Mairi.

"I don't have much experience with men," Fiona admitted. "I've been too busy, first with school and Mairi and then with my career, to pursue any serious relationships. Maybe I should keep it casual. Maybe we should just be friends."

"No, I didn't mean to warn you off. If you have feelings for my brother, go for it. I think you can make him happy."

Could she? She'd tried so hard, but had she ever made anyone happy?

"Feena!" Stella shouted as they approached the Delacroix family members milling around two picnic tables pushed together. The little girl pulled away from Amelia's handhold and ran through the light crowd to Fiona and Claire.

Fiona caught Stella and lifted her high in the air, making the little girl giggle. "What did your daddy and I say about holding on to someone's hand?"

The reprimand seemed to pop out of its own volition. Fiona's gaze shot to Stella's upturned face, and her tensed muscles relaxed. Her smile was just as wide as it had been. Fiona positioned her on her hip.

"Daddy holds hands so we no get lost."

Fiona stilled and hugged Stella to her. That pretty much summed things up. Fiona didn't feel lost when she had Marc and Stella beside her, and she was going to do everything she could to keep them there—for all their sakes.

"'Nuff hugs. Down. Where's Daddy?"

Fiona placed Stella on the floor in front of her and took her hand. "He'll be right here. He had to go to the car for something."

"Birthday present."

"Yes, and remember, no opening it until after we have supper and cake."

"I 'member. Let's eat."

"Slow down," Claire said. "We'll eat as soon as your daddy gets here."

The three of them walked to the tables, which Marc's mother had loaded with a variety of foods from the various vendors. A tall chocolate frosted cake with a number three candle on top stood front and center.

Fiona approached Marc's mother. "Did you have any trouble finding the cake?" she asked.

"No." Marc's mother tilted her head.

"I mean one that Stella can eat, that doesn't have…"

His mother's expression clouded at the same moment Fiona sensed Marc step behind her. She drew in and released a cleansing breath. She had to let her hypervigilance down, trust others, trust God as she was learning through Bridges. If she didn't let go of her old misplaced beliefs, she'd fail Marc, Stella and their family, as she'd failed her sisters.

A warm hand squeezed her shoulder and she gave Marc a crooked smile over her shoulder.

"No problem at all finding a cake," Marc's mother

answered belatedly. "Now everyone take their seats so we can say grace. We want to have time for the cake and ice cream before the fireworks start."

Fiona and Marc burst into laughter.

"What's so funny?"

"Inside joke," he said, gazing into Fiona's eyes with a warmth that turned her to mush.

"Come on, sit," Stella commanded, grabbing Fiona and Marc's hands and pulling them to an open spot at one of the tables.

Fiona slung her legs over the bench and sat, turning and reaching for Stella. "Need help up?"

"No, move. Daddy sit here." Stella pointed to the right of Fiona as she scrambled into the space on Fiona's left. "Big, bigger, biggest," she said.

Marc fit himself into the space Fiona had made, lining his leg up against hers. "I guess we know what the preschool class at The Kids Place studied this week."

"You've got it," Andie said from across the table. "And on this side of the table, we have small—" she pointed at herself "—smaller and smallest." She pointed at Aimee and Robbie beside her.

"No, Aunt Dee," Stella said, "you're big."

Everyone laughed as Fiona marveled at how much more at ease Stella was with Marc's family now, and how at ease she was.

"John, will you say grace?" Marc's mother said.

Marc enclosed her hand in his, and Fiona took Stella's.

"Dear Lord, first I want to thank you for this wonderful day and having all of our family here together..."

Fiona listened to Marc's father's words flow over her, leaving a shelter of peace around her.

"And let us accept Your will," Marc's father finished.

Fiona glanced through her eyelashes from Marc to Stella before adding her "amen."

"Happy birthday to you!" Oblivious to the people around them, Marc's family finished their enthusiastic birthday serenade to Stella.

"Now, blow out the candle."

Poof. Stella extinguished the flame and clapped her hands. "Present." She pointed at the wrapped gift Fiona had taken out of the bag and placed on the table in front of her.

"Yes, you can open Fiona's present," Marc said.

The rest of his family began pulling gifts from under the table. When his mother had said they'd celebrate with a cake here, he hadn't thought she meant a full-fledged birthday party. He had Stella's present, a tricycle, at the house to give her when they got home. Not that he would have lugged it here, but it would have been nice to know. Or had his mother told him? He'd been so wrapped up in work this week, he wasn't sure.

Fiona moved the gift in front of Stella, and she attacked the wrapping with an expression of anticipation that was duplicated on Fiona's face. A feeling he hadn't felt in a long time stirred in his chest.

"Elsa," Stella squealed.

"Yes, it's her castle," Fiona said, her eyes bright.

Stella scrambled onto Fiona's lap and handed him the plastic-encased toy. "Open, Daddy."

"First, tell Fiona thank you."

"Fank you, Feena."

"You're very welcome." Fiona's face still beamed.

"Now, I think it would be better if we waited until we're home to open Elsa's castle. We don't want to lose any pieces."

"Please," Stella begged.

"Go ahead, let her," his mother said. "It's not as if we have anything else to do until the fireworks start. You can take the other presents home if she doesn't get around to opening them."

Marc bristled at his mother contradicting him, and he did have something to do before the fireworks. While he'd waited for Stella and Fiona to finish having matching daisies painted on their cheeks, he'd run into the owner of one of the area apple orchards that he'd been trying to arrange a meeting with. He'd recognized the guy from the orchard's website and approached him. They made plans to meet near here in five minutes. Marc had figured that would give him plenty of time to be with Stella and Fiona for the fireworks.

He fidgeted on the hard bench. "I ran into the owner of Tripp's Orchards and told him I'd meet with him about now. I've been trying to connect with him about the orchard becoming a supplier for La Table Frais."

His mother drew her lips into a thin line.

"Go ahead," Fiona said. "I have you covered."

"Thanks." Marc waited for the brick sitting on his chest to lift, but it didn't completely. "I'll be back in plenty of time for the fireworks." He rose and stepped behind the table bench.

The smile Fiona gave him over her shoulder chipped a sizable chunk off the brick.

"Hand me that gift," his brother Paul said, his pocket jackknife already out to cut the plastic encasing the toy.

Stella's continued squeals about the toy turned Marc's feet to lead as he plodded toward the meeting place.

* * *

The crack of fireworks exploding outside the Armory after his meeting wiped out the euphoria of its success. He and the orchard owner had *not* finished in plenty of time to make the start of the display. Marc grabbed his coat from the coat check and pulled it on, making his way outside as quickly as he could without pushing people out of the way. Stella's only other experience with fireworks last Independence Day had terrified her, and he wasn't there with her. He couldn't remember if he'd told his mother or Fiona. He'd talked with Stella this morning about the fireworks and had expected to be with her when they started.

He paused outside, listening for Stella's frantic crying during the break between rockets. He didn't hear anything but the hum of the crowd talking. Scanning the area, he found his family front and center on the folding chairs arranged on the lawn. He rushed over.

"Daddy, fire!" Stella shouted as he made his way down the row to an empty seat next to Fiona. He searched Stella's face. There wasn't a tear in sight.

"Stella, she's okay?" He caught his breath and dropped into the chair. "I took her to the Fourth of July display last summer at the park near our old house, and it scared her so much we had to leave. I barely had her calmed down by the time we got home."

"She was frightened at first," his mother said, "but Fiona calmed her down."

"Thanks, but I should have been here," he said, regret lacing his words.

"All I did was distract her from the noise by pointing out the colors."

Another rocket exploded in the sky, and Marc tensed.

"Red, blue, green," Stella said.

His tension drained in increments with each color his daughter named. "I never thought of that."

"She probably didn't know her colors then, so it might not have worked," Fiona said.

Her words relieved most of his self-reproach that Fiona had been there for Stella and not him. He slid his arm across the back of Fiona's seat, curved his fingers around her shoulder and realized with a jolt that Fiona was his complement. The helpmate he'd thought he'd never find again, whom he hadn't even been looking for.

He bent his head to her ear. "I'm glad you're here," he whispered, pausing for a moment to breathe in the faint floral scent of her hair. "Not only for Stella. For me, too."

Fiona leaned toward him, her other shoulder warm against his. "I'm glad I'm here, too."

"More," Stella said after the finale finished.

"Sorry, sweetpea. That's it," he said.

She stuck out her bottom lip.

"We have an important job to do."

The lip came in.

"We need to get Fiona home safely. Can you help me do that?"

"Yes!" Stella bounced on Fiona's knee.

"Good save," Fiona said.

"Before you go," his mother said, "we have the presents in our car. Do you want to get them after church tomorrow?"

"That would be fine."

"And Fiona," she said, "you're welcome to join us for church. Service is at ten thirty."

"Church. Sing," Stella said.

"I'd like you to come," he said. "If you want. Stella and I could pick you up since your car isn't running."

"I've been thinking about trying a service. I…my family…we weren't big churchgoers."

"Sorry if I put you on the spot," Marc's mother apologized.

"No, I'd like to come."

Marc squeezed Fiona's shoulder. "Good. Now, we have a birthday girl we need to get home. See you all tomorrow."

As seemed to be the usual, by the time they were a couple miles outside of Ticonderoga, Stella was fast asleep.

"I want to apologize, too," Marc said.

Fiona's eyes and forehead crinkled exactly like Stella's did when she was trying to figure out something, drawing him to her.

He caught himself veering toward the shoulder of the road and corrected his course.

"For what?" she asked.

"It's the weekend. Family time. I shouldn't have spent so long talking with Tom Tripp. But we'd been playing phone tag all week."

"It's okay. This time," she teased.

Or at least he thought it was teasing. Although her cheeks dimpled, Marc caught an undercurrent of truth to her words.

"I know," he said. "I appreciate that. No, more than that, I like knowing you're around to back me up. We make a good team, and I don't just mean you and me and Stella. I mean you and me without Stella, too. I like having you around." He pulled off his ski cap. "I mean, I care for you. A lot." He rubbed his back against the seat. "I'm messing this up, aren't I?"

"No." She smiled. "You're doing fine. I like knowing I'm not only a backup for Stella's care."

"Definitely not." His gaze caught and held hers for a moment too long, and the car swerved to the right. Marc's heart pounded with a shot of adrenaline from the realization he'd let the distraction that was Fiona affect his driving again. "We'll pick this up when we get to your place."

Fiona glanced by him to Stella in the back.

"She's probably out for the night," he said.

Fiona rolled her lips in and released them. "About Stella's care. We need to be a team, share the responsibility equally. I can't take the majority of it."

The temperature in the car dropped a few degrees. "I wouldn't ask you to." Marc tried to ignore the unreadable play of emotions on her face and bring back the warm joy of a few minutes ago.

"So." Fiona folded her hands in her lap and looked up at him expectantly when he parked the SUV in her driveway ten minutes later. Her earnest look invited back all the warm feelings that had jumbled his thoughts earlier.

"I'll walk you to your door."

Stella rustled in the back seat, and they turned to her simultaneously.

"What if she wakes up and you're not here?" Fiona asked.

He'd only be twenty feet away, but he appreciated her concern for Stella. "At least let me impress you with the gentlemanly manners my mother and sisters drilled into me and get the car door for you."

Fiona waited while he got out and walked around the front of the vehicle. He opened her door and bowed. "Your home, my lady."

Her mouth twitched, drawing his attention to her lips. "Very impressive."

He couldn't agree more. Marc took her hand, and she stepped out and into his arms as if they'd both planned it. Her warmth—or was it his?—radiated through the layers of their outerwear as he lowered his mouth to hers and drank in Fiona's sweetness and the feeling that he'd come home after a long journey. He lifted his head and savored the serene expression on her face.

Fiona bustled around her apartment one last time, making sure everything was ready for her, Marc and Stella's movie date and hummed one of the hymns they'd sung together at the church service this morning. Her alto had blended with Marc's rich tenor, making her spirits soar with the music.

After the wonderful day she'd had yesterday and the equally wonderful way it had ended, Fiona had been hesitant about going through with her agreement to join the Delacroixs at church this morning. What if, as had too often been the story of her life, the enchantment of the moonlit kiss she had Marc had shared was gone with the morning light and reality of everyday life?

But rather than feeling an outsider at the Hazardtown Community Church service, Fiona had felt part of the Delacroix family and in the company of friends, even though she'd met many of the parishioners for the first time at the coffee hour fellowship after the service.

Stop, she told herself as she repositioned the throw pillows on the couch for the third time, imagining her, Marc and Stella cuddled there watching *Frozen*. Before she began believing in a warm family future for the three of them, she and Marc needed to have the talk they hadn't had last night before kissing good-night. She touched her finger to her lips, remembering the soft sensation of his lips touching hers, before she mentally chided herself for thinking like a moonstruck teen-ager. Stella had been up late yesterday and up early for church. Maybe she'd drift off after the movie and din-ner, giving her and Marc time to talk.

A light knock sounded at the door before she had to look for another outlet for her nervous energy. Fiona opened the door to Stella standing on the top step clutching a DVD to her chest and Marc at the bottom.

"I'm here," Stella announced.

"So you are. Come in."

"Daddy get food."

Marc waved up the stairwell. "I'll be right back."

Fiona closed the door and turned to Stella, who still clutched the DVD to herself with one hand while she pulled at the zipper of her coat with the other one. Her face scrunched in concentration. Or was it frustration? Fiona couldn't tell.

"Let me help you." Somewhere in the back of her mind she seemed to remember Marc saying it was bet-ter to tell or direct Stella than ask her questions.

Stella released her breath in a puff. "'Kay."

Fiona made a little bit of a show of the zipper being sticky. "There you go. Now, give me your hat and gloves and coat, and I'll put them on the chair."

It was silly and more than a little childish, but if Stella's outerwear was on the recliner, Marc would have no choice but to sit with her and Stella on the couch to watch the movie.

"You can put your movie on the table next to the TV," Fiona said.

"No, wait for Daddy."

A thump at the door signaled his return.

"It's open," Fiona called.

"I don't have any free hands."

"We'd better go help him."

Fiona opened the door and relieved Marc of one of the covered dishes he was carrying.

He closed the door behind him with his foot. "I've got meat loaf with oven-roasted potatoes, onions and carrots. It's one of the dishes that I want to offer as local fare at La Table Frais."

Her shoulders knotted. Today was about them, as a family, as a couple. Fiona pushed his mention of the restaurant out of her mind. "So we're the guinea pigs?" She motioned at herself and Stella.

"I'm not a pig," Stella protested.

Fiona and Marc laughed.

"You certainly aren't," Fiona said. "I meant your daddy has us testing his recipe."

Confusion colored Stella's face.

"Never mind, sweetpea. You and Fiona can put in the movie while I put our dinner in the oven. I prepared it at home, so I wouldn't be stuck in the kitchen slaving over a hot stove while you two were enjoying the movie."

"I thought you'd already seen the movie," Fiona said.

"But you haven't," he said. "I want to see you enjoy every moment of it."

Fiona's earlier nervous energy changed into a different sensation that was nonetheless agitating.

"You wouldn't happen to have any popcorn I could make while I'm in the kitchen, do you?" he asked. "You can't watch a movie without something to munch on."

"No, I didn't think that was a good choice." Fiona tilted her head toward Stella, feeling the weight of a vigilance that she felt Marc didn't take seriously. "But when you come back out, you can bring the hummus and crackers I got."

"On it." He appeared unaffected by her admonishment. "Go ahead. Put the movie in."

"No, wait for you, Daddy," Stella said, her bright gaze darting around the room and settling on a farm and game magazine on the coffee table. She picked it up and handed it to Fiona before settling herself on the couch. "Story."

"Have fun with that," Marc said, disappearing into her kitchen.

Fiona sat next to Stella, who snuggled into her side, triggering a bittersweet memory of her as a nine- or ten-year-old reading to Mairi and Beth on the couch because their mother "had to go out." She spread the magazine open to an article on sheep farming and placed her arm around her niece. Stella would never want for her love and security as Fiona and her sisters had wanted for their parents' love.

"And this baby lamb was born a triplet with a sister and a brother, but the mommy sheep could only feed two of them, so the farmer's big girl fed the third lamb from a baby bottle." Fiona pointed to a photo of a teen feeding a lamb.

"The baby lamb is 'dopted like me."

"I guess she is."

"My mommy's in heaven," Stella said.

Fiona didn't know where that had come from. "I know."

"I like your stories. You could 'dopt me like Daddy."

Fiona's chest squeezed with longing. It was too soon. She couldn't allow herself to dream in the direction of being more than an aunt to Stella. Before she could speak, Fiona caught a motion out of the corner of her eye. *Marc*. Despite having done nothing to encourage

Stella's thought, Fiona's cheeks colored. How long had he been standing there? How much had he heard?

Fiona closed the magazine and put it back on the table. Marc set down the hummus and crackers without saying anything.

"Daddy." Stella picked up the DVD from the couch cushion beside her. "Movie in."

"Hmm. I'm not sure I can. What's that word I need to give me the power?"

"Please!" Stella shouted. "Feena, too."

"Please," Fiona repeated.

"That's my girls."

Fiona relaxed, allowing herself to bask in the warmth of feeling like she belonged.

Marc started the DVD and walked back to join them. "Slide down, Stella, so I can sit next to Fiona."

"Big, bigger, biggest," he said when Stella made no effort to move.

She rolled over to the far side of the couch. "Big, bigger, biggest."

Marc settled in with them and put his arm behind her on the back of the couch. "My partners think they've found the sous-chef for La Table Frais," he said over the credits and previews playing on the TV. "If she's half as good as she looks on paper, she might be able to take over the restaurant once I get it going."

"Meaning?" Fiona didn't want to talk business. She wanted this time to be the Sunday family time Marc had talked about. But she needed to know what he meant.

"That if I wanted to, I could consider returning to the New York City restaurant. Stella and I have made real progress since we've been here, and it wouldn't be right away."

"Oh." Her surprise rounded her mouth into a circle

that she quickly snapped shut so she didn't look as foolish as she felt.

"Daddy, quiet. Please. *Frozen*."

"I'll be quiet. But think about it, Fiona."

Fiona had only an inkling of what he wanted her to think about, but she let it drop for now and got into the movie with Stella who, to Fiona's delight, acted as the self-appointed commentator.

Near the end of the movie, Marc's phone buzzed. He took it from his pocket. Concern creased his handsome face. "I'd better take this. Sorry." He stood and headed toward the kitchen, leaving a chasm of coolness where he'd been sitting.

When the movie finished, Stella scrambled onto Fiona's lap. "Did you love it, Feena?"

"I loved it."

Stella hugged her. "I love you."

Fiona's heart soared. "I love you, too, sweetie." Then it plummeted as it hit her that against her better judgment and despite all the protective walls she'd built, she was falling in love with the little girl's father, too.

"I've got to go," Marc said, reaching for his coat on the chair. "It looks like someone broke into the restaurant. You two go ahead and eat, and I'll be back as quickly as I can."

He kissed first Stella, and then Fiona, on the forehead.

"Daddy work?" Stella asked.

"Yes, he has to go to work for a while." The words tasted bitter in her mouth. It wasn't Marc's fault. He was a lot closer than his partners. But today was family day.

"Feena no work."

"No, I don't have to work."

A couple hours later, after Fiona and Stella had eaten and Stella had fallen asleep on the couch, Marc called.

"Hey." His deep voice rolled over her. "I'm at the police station. I'm going to have to stick around a while longer. Sorry. I called Mom, and she'll come get Stella and keep her overnight."

"I could have kept her." Did her words sound as plaintive to Marc as they did to her?

"I didn't want to take advantage of you. Stella has clothes at Mom's and is used to being there on Monday mornings. You know. Toddlers and routines." He forced a laugh.

"Right." This was what she wanted. Not to have to pick up on Marc's responsibilities if he fell down on them.

What was wrong with her? He wasn't falling down on his responsibility to Stella. He couldn't help the break-in.

"I'll talk to you tomorrow." Marc's voice dropped lower. "You don't know how much I wish I was there."

"Oh, I might."

"Bye."

Fiona placed her phone on the end table beside her and rested her hand on it. Her thoughts and her emotions were all jumbled. Did she even know what love was? Did she have it in her to give or receive it? Could she explain her feelings to Marc?

Maybe with help. She picked up her phone and tapped her email icon. They could meet with Noah. Participating in his email meditation group for spiritual guidance had helped her start applying her new faith to her life. But she still needed support. With Noah in the room, she could lay out her fears and wants to Marc coherently without her growing attraction to him interfering, urging her to put off talking because of what it would reveal about her.

Gazing at Stella fast asleep, Fiona felt a weight lift, and hope filled the gap. She'd make things right. They'd work it out.

Chapter Twelve

Hey, I'm cutting out of work early. I'll pick up Stella and meet you at your house when you get home.

Fiona shot the text off to Marc. The temperature forecast for today was seventy degrees, almost unheard of for March in this area, and she was going to make the most of the unseasonable warmth. She'd pick up Stella from his oldest sister's house where his nieces were watching her and swing by the grocery store to buy fixings for a picnic. It could make up for the time together they'd lost on Sunday. She sang along with the car radio. And if the temperature dropped too much by the time Marc got home, they could picnic inside.

She pulled into the driveway of a neat ranch house set in a stand of pines, pastures fanning out behind a red barn.

Stella darted out of the house toward the car to meet her.

She cranked the engine off and jumped out, her heart banging on her chest wall. Where were the twins?

"Daddy?" Stella looked at the car and the road.

"Still working."

A breathless Amelia joined them. "I'm sorry. The door was locked. She saw you drive in from the window. I told her to wait, said you'd be in in a minute. I guess she unlocked the door."

Fiona counted to five to control her anger. She hadn't been much older than Amelia when her mother had died and she'd been Mairi's guardian. "You guess?" Her voice shook a little. "Never underestimate a toddler."

"I said I'm sorry. It won't happen again."

That's right, it wouldn't. Because if Fiona had any say, she wouldn't be watching Stella again.

Fiona squatted to Stella's level. "Sweetie, I'm glad to see you, too, but you should never run into the driveway when a car is pulling in. Never." She pulled her niece into a tight hug.

"'Nuff." Stella pushed away, and Fiona released her grip. The little girl grabbed her hand and pulled her toward the house. "See my paintings."

Amelia trudged behind them. Had she been too hard on the teen? No, Amelia should have seen Stella fiddling with the door lock.

Aimee met them at the door.

"You locked the door after you brought the mail in, didn't you?" Amelia said.

"Yes." Aimee paused. "I think so. I was so excited when I saw the acceptance package from SUNY Geneseo." She turned to Fiona. "It's my first-choice college."

"The front door, the one facing the road, wasn't locked?"

Both teens hung their heads. Fiona couldn't help mentally blaming them.

"My painting." Stella tugged at her pant leg. "In the kitchen."

Her niece's insistence stopped Fiona from saying

anything more to the twins. Amelia led them into the spotless room.

Guilt about her earlier harshness toward the twins washed over Fiona. The girls had obviously cleaned up after what Fiona was sure had been a messy painting session. What kid didn't make a mess finger painting?

"Here." Stella pulled Fiona to the table and pointed at three finger paintings. "Dry?" the little girl asked.

"They should be," Amelia said. "Stella made them after lunch, before her nap."

Fiona glanced at Stella. And they'd cleaned up Stella, too, possibly even changed her clothes, since Fiona didn't see any paint on her.

"Wow! Nice job cleaning up," Fiona said, still feeling small about her earlier criticisms. But the unlocked front door could have put Stella in danger.

The twins stared at her for a moment before shrugging their shoulders and mumbling, "Thanks."

Stella touched the paint on one of the pictures. "All dry." She picked it up. "For Daddy."

"Do you want to give it to me to take to Daddy?" Fiona asked. "We're going to go to the store to buy things for a surprise picnic for him at your house." Fiona held her breath while Stella digested what she'd said.

The little girl cocked her head. "You, me, Daddy?"

"Yes."

"With cookies?"

"We could buy some cookies."

Stella's expression turned serious. "Aimee and 'Melia said no cookies for snack."

"What did you have for a snack?" Fiona eyed the jar of crunchy peanut butter on the counter. Marc would have told the twins about Stella's food restrictions, wouldn't he?

"Crackers and jam."

"What kind of jam?" Fiona asked Amelia.

"Apricot. Why?"

Fiona released her breath in relief. "Stella shouldn't have any berry jams that might have seeds in them. Didn't your uncle leave you a list of Stella's food restrictions?"

Amelia shrugged. "He said no apples, unless we peeled them, and nothing with nuts. He was in a rush when he dropped Stella off. Some kind of meeting or something he had to get to."

A spark of anger lit inside Fiona. Stella's health was more important than any meeting he had to get to. Marc couldn't be that casual when it came to Stella's food restrictions. Not if he wanted to keep her symptoms in remission. Fiona took a deep breath to calm herself. She'd talk to Marc again. She'd told him that she'd say something if he was putting work first, and she would.

"Here," Stella said, pulling her from her thoughts. Her niece handed her the painting she'd made for her father and picked up another of the pictures. "Gammy's."

"You can leave that here if you want," Amelia said. "My mom will see Grandma at choir practice tonight."

"'Kay." Stella picked up her last painting. "Feena's," she said with a dimpled smile that melted through Fiona.

She took the picture. "Very nice. Thank you."

"Stella, Daddy and Feena." The little girl pointed to each of the three stick figures holding hands. "Aimee helped me."

"Stella wanted to include the whole family. We told her that would take several pictures to fit them all." Amelia laughed. "So she picked you and Uncle Marc." Amelia raised an eyebrow in a look so much like the ones Fiona had received from Marc's mother when she'd referred to the two of them as a couple that Fiona almost burst out laughing.

"My family," Stella said, patting the paper.

"Let's get going," she said to try to calm all the different emotions swirling inside her. "Where's your stuff?"

"In my packpack." Stella scampered off.

"It's in the living room," Amelia said. "Uncle Marc didn't leave her car seat for the car, though."

"That's okay. I have one."

Amelia gave her the eyebrow lift again. The first time it was cute. The second verged on irritating. She'd had too many assumptions made about her in the past, and had too many disappointments when she'd allowed herself to accept people's hopes for her.

Fiona stopped midstep. Maybe her irritation was misdirected. She was irritated at Marc rather than his niece because he hadn't made time for her—or Stella—this week.

Fiona got Stella out to the car, and they made quick work of picking out their picnic food at the store. In the checkout line, Stella scrunched her face as if in pain.

"What's wrong, sweetpea?" Marc's pet name came naturally.

"Potty."

The last person ahead of them finished. "We're almost done. Can you wait a minute?"

"No!" Stella shouted. "My tummy hurts."

Fiona lifted Stella from the cart seat and looked at the woman behind the checkout counter. "I'm going to push my cart out of the way so the others can go ahead, and I'll come back."

"Sure," the woman said, and Fiona dashed for the ladies' room at the back of the store.

"Hurts," Stella whimpered as Fiona cranked open the door, transported to another time and another little girl—Beth. She and Mairi had come home from school to their mother passed out in the bedroom and Beth crying uncontrollably in the bathroom from a combination of pain and fear of being disciplined for having an accident. She'd done the best she could for Beth. She'd do better for Stella.

"I want my daddy!" Stella screamed, tears rolling down her baby cheeks.

Someone knocked on the stall door. Fiona hadn't even heard anyone come in. "Is everything okay?" a voice asked.

"Yes, she's not feeling well. We'll be out in a minute."

"Do you need me to get someone? The emergency squad?"

"My daddy," Stella sobbed.

Fiona hesitated a moment. "No, thanks. I'm her aunt. I'm trying to get ahold of her father."

She pressed Marc's number. Her phone rang a couple of times before it clicked to an out-of-service area message. Where was his meeting? The question rang in her ears. Despite a new cell tower in the area, there were still a lot of pockets in the mountains with no cell service.

"Daddy?" Stella's voice had turned plaintive.

"No, I didn't get through, sweetpea. If you're done, I'm going to take you home and call him again."

"Home." Stella sniffed.

Fiona felt every eye in the store on her as she carried Stella past the checkout. "I'm sorry, I don't need the groceries."

"Hope everything is okay," the cashier said with a sympathetic smile.

The glass exit door opened. Maybe she should have accepted help, let the woman who'd come into the restroom call the emergency squad. But her parents' lectures and reprimands had wired her to avoid letting people know any family business.

Her foot caught on the metal threshold strip when she stepped out. Fiona tightened her grasp on the door with one hand and her grip on Stella with her other, drawing the little girl closer to her heart while she steadied her footing. Stella threw her arms around her and buried her face in Fiona's shoulder. She needed to get in touch with Marc, to find out what he wanted her to do.

Once in her car, Fiona tried Marc again and got the same message. She turned the key, and Stella cried out above the hum of the engine.

"It's okay, sweetpea. Daddy will be home soon."

"N'kay. It hurts." Stella burst into loud, pain-laced tears. "Bad apples. Stella not bad." She lapsed into baby talk.

Fiona unbuckled her seatbelt and turned in her seat to stroke Stella's cheek. "Of course you're not bad. Did Aimee or Amelia give you an apple?"

"One."

Amelia had said Marc told them to peel any apples they gave the girl, but she had to ask anyway. "Did she peel it?"

Stella scrunched her little face in disdain. "Yes, and said no more apples." The little girl dropped her head to her chest. "I took free. Put them in Kanga's pocket."

Stella's stuffed kangaroo. Fiona swallowed the painful lump in her throat. *Three?* But everything was three to Stella.

"You ate them?"

Stella nodded. "Hurts." She pressed her tummy and resumed crying.

"I know. I'm going to try to call your daddy again." Fiona dug in her purse. She had to do something. Stella's discomfort was breaking her heart. In a side pocket, she found what she was looking for—the number to La Table Frais that she'd meant to add to her phone contacts. Maybe Marc was there now, or they could give her a number other than his cell where she could reach him.

On the ninth ring, when Fiona was about to hang up, a male voice answered the restaurant phone. "Sean?" Fiona recognized his voice. "This is Fiona. Is Marc there, or do you know where I can reach him? His cell is out of service."

"No. He left before lunch. I heard him say something about meeting with the partners about the new chef they're hiring. I don't have a number. Sorry."

Neither did she. "All right. Thanks." She pressed end.

Marc went down to New York? He hadn't said anything to her. If it was spur of the moment, wouldn't he have called his nieces to let them know? They hadn't said anything to her about Marc being late. Fiona dropped her head to the steering wheel. *What should I do?*

Stella hiccupped. "Pray, Jesus."

Fiona's head shot up. She must have spoken her thought. Fiona had let too many disappointments in life put her out of the habit of expecting answers to prayer. But praying might calm her and allow her to think rationally, rather than with her emotions as she was now. She bowed her head.

Dear Lord, out of the mouth of babes, You have given strength. Let me use that strength to believe and see Your answer. Amen.

Fiona lifted her head and checked the clock on the dashboard. Not quite five.

Then it hit her. Dr. Franklin—she had his card in her purse and his office would still be open.

Marc whistled as he walked the shoveled path to his sister Andie's house. Everything was falling into place. He and his partners had found the perfect second-in-command chef for La Table Frais. They'd come up to Albany this afternoon so they could all conduct a final interview with her. After the interview, he'd been able to report to his partners that the renovations were ahead of schedule and the other arrangements for the opening were on schedule.

The extra hours he'd put in these past few weeks, personally meeting with the contacts Fiona and her program had put him in touch with, had paid off. He scratched his earlobe. He'd make it up to Stella—and Fiona—for the time he'd missed out with them. He'd hardly talked with Fiona in the past week, and when he had, it had been business. Driving to his various meetings had given him time to think. He was ready and eager to devote a lot more time to their personal relationship.

"Hi, Uncle Marc." His nephew Robbie looked up from the game he was playing on a tablet. "What are you doing here?"

"I'm here to pick up Stella."

"She's not here." He went back to his game.

Not here? "Did the girls take her outside?" They better not have driven her anywhere. He'd purposely not left her car seat because he wasn't comfortable with the teens taking her out in the car in the snow. Andie knew that, if Aimee and Amelia didn't. But Andie's car wasn't in the driveway. Although it could be in the garage. He scratched his head. Robbie was here, so she must have come home from work at The Kids Place.

Robbie shrugged.

"Marc." His sister walked in. "I thought I heard your voice. Didn't Fiona get a hold of you?"

"No. But my phone's been wonky since yesterday, giving me out-of-service messages when I should have service. I was too busy to stop in the phone store in Ticonderoga, and my meeting in Albany lasted longer than I thought it would."

"Fiona picked up Stella about 3:30. Maybe I shouldn't tell you."

He frowned at her. "You should tell me everything about Stella."

"Amelia said Fiona was planning a surprise picnic at your house."

A weight lifted from him. He should have known it was something like that. Marc looked out the window at the waning sunlight. "I'd better head home and see if they've saved me any food."

Andie laughed. "I'm sure they have. Enjoy your evening."

"I plan to."

Andie gave him a knowing look, but he didn't care. He enjoyed being with Fiona in whatever they were doing, and Stella was accepting Fiona into her life, too.

When he got to his house, the driveway was empty and no lights were on inside. Maybe Andie had gotten the details from the twins wrong, and Fiona had taken Stella to her house. She didn't have a yard for a picnic, but the park was close by her apartment. He relaxed back into the seat and texted Fiona. When he didn't get a quick response, he called her. After a short ring, he got an out-of-service message. He clicked the phone off and tossed it into the passenger's seat. He had to make time to get it fixed or replaced.

A few minutes later he pulled into Fiona's driveway, but saw no car there and no lights on inside. He slapped the top of the steering wheel. Where were they? He picked up his phone and texted his sister.

Are the twins there?

Yes.

Now the phone was working.

Keep them there. I'm coming back. Fiona and Stella aren't at my house or hers.

Marc tried texting and calling Fiona again with the same results. He pulled back onto Main Street and gunned the engine when he hit the village limits. Rationally, he knew there was some logical explanation as to where Fiona and Stella were, but all he could think was that an accident of some sort might have happened.

Marc screeched to a halt in Andie's driveway. His mom. Fiona might have called her if she hadn't been able to get a hold of him. Once Mom had made her one-eighty about accepting Fiona, she'd treated her as another daughter—or daughter-in-law. Mom seemed to think of him, Fiona and Stella as one unit lately.

He called his mother from the car.

"Hi, Mom. By any chance are Fiona and Stella there?"

She laughed. "Lost your girls? That's what you get for neglecting them."

"Mom, I'm serious, and I haven't neglected them. I've just been busier with work lately. They're there, aren't they?"

"No, they're not."

His phone beeped. "I've got a call, Mom. Hang on while I take it." He glanced at the number, which he didn't recognize, and, heart thumping in his throat, answered.

"Mr. Delacroix?" a man said.

"Yes." Marc squeezed the phone.

"This is James Fry, from the Schroon Lake Pharmacy. I have the prescription for Stella Delacroix that Dr. Franklin's office called in this evening. It's ready for pickup. If you want to stop by tonight, we're open until nine."

"What prescription?"

The pharmacy assistant rattled off a medication he'd never heard of.

"Dr. Franklin sent it today?"

"Yes, about an hour ago." Impatience crept into the pharmacy assistant's voice.

"All right. Thank you. I'm not sure I can make it in tonight. I'll pick it up first thing in the morning." Right now, he had to find Stella and Fiona.

"We'll see you then." The pharmacy assistant clicked off.

"Mom, you still there?"

"I'm here. Was that Fiona?"

"No, it was the pharmacy with a new prescription for Stella." He told her the name.

"Dr. Franklin mentioned that when I took Stella for her appointment. I may not have mentioned it because he wanted to wait and see if it was needed before he prescribed it."

"Then why did he prescribe it now?" he said in a strained voice.

"I don't know. I'm surprised Fiona didn't call you."

Mom's not the only one. He bit his tongue so he didn't take his frustration out on his mother. "She might have. My phone hasn't been working right. But when Fiona couldn't reach me, she could have called you instead of taking things into her own hands."

"Yeah, I'm a little surprised she didn't. But she's taken on a lot of responsibility for Stella the past couple weeks. I'll text her now."

Marc didn't know if that was a dig or his guilty conscience overreacting. But his current workload was temporary, and he was still Stella's *father*, even if he'd signed the consent forms for Fiona to seek treatment for Stella.

"If Fiona had tried to reach you and couldn't, she may feel comfortable going with her own judgment."

Marc wasn't as sure. At times, it seemed Fiona couldn't separate Stella's condition from her baby sister Beth's. She needed to embrace the faith he knew she had inside her and let go of the shell of fear that colored her perception of Stella's health and what needed to be done. Couldn't she see that they, together with his family, had things in hand?

He rubbed his chest. From what he'd gathered, her role model for mothering was a woman who ran toward an elusive "something better" whenever she faced a family challenge, leaving Fiona to be the adult in the family, the one who took control. But Stella wasn't Beth, and Fiona wasn't the only one able to take proper care of Stella. While the rational side of him knew he should be happy to have her act proactively if something was wrong with Stella, he couldn't stop the resentment boiling inside him.

Marc bit his tongue so he didn't take that resentment out on his mother. "I'm at Andie's. I'm going to talk with Aimee and Amelia to see if Stella wasn't feeling well. All I can figure is Fiona took Stella to see Dr. Franklin." He didn't want to think about the other possibilities bouncing around in his head.

"And I'll try again in a bit to get a hold of Fiona and get back to you if I do. You let me know if you find something out first. I'll be praying."

"Thanks, Mom." And he'd be praying there was no reason for praying.

Andie met him as soon as he walked in. "I talked with Aimee and Amelia."

"And?" He yanked down the zipper of his jacket.

"I'm going to let them tell you."

Marc shoved his hand through his hair. He could understand the value of having teens take responsibility for their actions, but Andie had kids. She should know how anxious he was to get any information about where Fiona and Stella were.

"They're in the dining room," Andie said, following him in.

Aimee and Amelia sat on the far side of the big maple table, looking like suspects in a TV crime show waiting to be interrogated. For a second, he wondered if he was the good cop or the bad cop.

He pulled out a chair across from them. "Do you guys know where Fiona took Stella?" He rubbed his palm on his pant leg. He'd made it sound like Fiona had kidnapped Stella or something.

They shook their heads in unison, and Amelia said,

"Fiona told Stella they were going to make a picnic at your house."

"And Mom said we should tell you that Stella said her tummy hurt a while after she got up from her nap," Amelia and.

"You didn't let her eat anything I said she couldn't have, did you?" He should have written down the list for them.

"She wanted an apple with lunch, so I peeled one like you told us to." Aimee picked at the purple polish on her nails.

"That's good," he reassured her.

"When Stella finished, she begged for another, but I told her not now. She tried to take one from the bowl. I told her no and asked her if she wanted to finger-paint to distract her."

"And?"

Amelia jumped in. "After Fiona picked up Stella, I found two apple cores and a wrapper from a granola bar under my bed. Aimee had left the box of peanut crunch granola bars out on the table." She gave her twin a pointed look.

"And Amelia wasn't watching Stella closely and let her open the front door and run outside to meet Fiona."

"Girls," Andie warned. "We're trying to help Uncle Marc, not place blame on each other." She shot him a sympathetic look. "I tried to call Fiona, but it went to voice mail. I left her a message and a text."

The knot in his stomach tightened. Fiona wouldn't have handled the twins' lack of supervision well, although he suspected she'd been left in far more dangerous situations at Stella's age.

Amelia didn't let it drop. "You were the one who probably left the door unlocked, and Fiona already read me the riot act on that one. You would have thought I had put Stella in danger on purpose. Nothing bad happened."

Marc raised his hand as the teens glared at each other. "Both the apple peels and nuts and fiber in the granola bars could have upset Stella's stomach. Did you tell Fiona that Stella didn't feel well?" Fiona tended toward hypervigilant. That might have prompted her to take things into her own hands and call Dr. Franklin.

"I didn't," Amelia said.

"Me, neither," Aimee answered.

"It doesn't matter. Thanks, Andie, girls. I'm going to call Stella's doctor and find out if Fiona took her up to his office in Saranac Lake this afternoon." Although if she had, they should have been back by now, unless Stella had been admitted to the hospital.

He clenched his fists under the table. If Dr. Franklin had sent them to the medical center in Saranac Lake, Fiona should have contacted him. His phone was working now. Unless, through her family filters, Fiona thought she needed to protect Stella because he and the twins were neglecting her. But Fiona had repeatedly said all she wanted was to be Stella's aunt.

Then a bunch of memories rushed in at once. The carnival. Admitting his feelings to Fiona. What he'd thought was her reciprocal admission. The way they meshed, and she always backed him up with Stella.

What had happened today that Fiona hadn't trusted the family or him for help? His head and heart ached with unanswered questions.

Chapter Thirteen

Fiona carried an exhausted Stella from the medical center to the car and buckled her into her seat, blinking away the juxtaposition of Beth's features on Stella's drowsy face. The medication Dr. Franklin had given Stella had finally calmed her. Fiona pushed the door closed so as not to disturb Stella and dragged herself into the driver's seat. Between her own fears and the strain of trying to comfort Stella while they waited for the results of the test the doctor had ordered, Fiona was as drained as the little girl.

She checked her phone for cell reception and anything from Marc before starting the car. Still nothing. Fiona started the car and headed toward the Northway to take Stella home. Dr. Franklin had ordered the ultrasound Stella had been scheduled to have next week. Fiona wanted to share with Marc that the doctor had found no blockage—her greatest fear. A blockage had been the beginning of Beth's decline. But would Marc even understand the importance of that? He'd been slow to read the information on the websites Dr. Franklin had recommended and to accept Stella's illness. Fiona rolled her head against her shoulders to relieve the tightness in her neck that was triggering a headache.

The doctor had found signs of inflammation, though. Inflammation that had probably been there before Stella had eaten the apples and granola that had aggravated it. How had Marc missed that? Stella must have shown signs, said something, and he'd ignored it. The voice of a younger Fiona spoke through the growing pain of her headache. *He hasn't lived through this before. Like Dad, he doesn't want to see it. But someone has to.*

A couple miles outside of Saranac Lake, her phone buzzed with a call, and her already racing heart picked up tempo. The snow banks on either side of the road left no shoulder to pull off on, so she couldn't take the call, not while driving with Stella in the car. Fiona glanced at the number. The call was from Marc's mother, not him. But he was Stella's father. She was his responsibility, not his mother's.

As she approached the entrance to the Northway, her phone buzzed again. This time, it was Andie. The call was followed by a text. Fiona saw the turn for the on-ramp and drove by it, heading east toward Burlington, Vermont, away from Paradox Lake and the Delacroixs. Andie and his mother couldn't cover for him, like she couldn't cover for her negligent mother when she was a child, as much as she'd tried to. But she was an adult now.

"Daddy," Stella murmured.

Fiona shot a glance over her shoulder. The little girl appeared to still be fast asleep.

Fiona slowed the car for the lower speed limit in Westport, a sick feeling spreading through her. If she was an adult, why was she punishing Marc and his family by not taking Stella home, not pulling over to take their calls? Because she was acting on old instinct, running like her mother had whenever her hard life got harder.

But she wasn't her mother. She had everything she wanted in Paradox Lake—family and the love of a good man, if Marc and the Delacroixs would still have her, and her work. She swallowed her nausea. Her impulsive reaction today had probably ruined any legal avenues she might pursue for visitation with Stella if Marc chose to withhold it. So she had to depend on Marc's forgiveness.

Her phone pinged again with a text from Marc, and she immediately pulled to the curb.

Where are you? Are you and Stella all right?

Westport, she texted. She'd explain when she saw him. Stella is okay.

As for herself, Fiona wasn't sure she was okay or ever would be. This whole disaster was her own fault—for letting the past, her fears and that crazy instinct to run consume her. That's why she'd never pursued romantic or family relationships. Despite the acceptance by the Delacroixs as family, obviously she still didn't know how to do family and love.

On our way home, she texted before turning the phone off. What she needed to say had to be said in person.

It was nearly ten o'clock when Fiona pulled into Marc's driveway. He was out of the house and beside her before she had even finished unbuckling Stella from her car seat. Tall and strong, with a rawness in his expression that made her heart bleed.

"I'll get her," he said, stepping between her and

Stella. He lifted the little girl out of the car and hugged her close to him without waking her. "You said she's okay. I got a call from the pharmacy about a prescription."

"Yes, to calm the irritation." Fiona shivered. While still warm for March, the evening temperature had dropped well below the afternoon high, and she wore only a spring jacket. "Can we go inside and talk?"

Marc's hesitation drove a stake through her heart.

"Yes, you need to fill me in on what Dr. Franklin said."

And a lot more if he'd let her. She followed him into the house.

"I'm going to put Stella to bed."

He went upstairs, leaving Fiona to pace his living room, straining to hear if Stella woke up. She prayed not. She needed to have her say before she left. Marc returned a few minutes later, and she handed him the printouts from the doctor's visit and emergency room that she'd grabbed from her car. Fiona shifted her weight from foot to foot as he read it.

"Sit down." His tone lightened. "Please."

She perched on the edge of the recliner, not allowing herself the intimacy of sharing the couch with him.

He dropped onto the couch. "Why?" He lifted his hands helplessly.

She picked at a rough edge on her thumb cuticle. "We went to the store to get the food for the picnic. Stella was crying. She was in pain. The twins were so casual about what they'd fed Stella. The front door wasn't locked. Stella ran out." She knew her words were jumbled. They made little sense to her, so she was sure they didn't make any to Marc.

"Breathe," he said, a gentle command.

He doesn't hate me, the little girl inside her said.

"I was scared. I imagined the worst, a blockage. That's how Beth's decline started."

"Stella isn't Beth. You could have contacted me."

"I tried." She dragged out her phone for the text she'd sent and stared at it, heart sinking, before showing him the words. "But I sent it to the wrong person."

"It didn't raise a red flag when I didn't respond?" A muscle worked in his jaw.

She leaned forward. "It did. I called you and didn't get through, so I called the restaurant. Sean said you were with your partners interviewing the chef candidate. I didn't know when you'd get back from New York City. I had to do something. I called Dr. Franklin's office."

"I was in Albany, not New York. I could have been back in an hour." His voice was flat. "You should have called my mother or Connor. They would have let me know, and he would have driven to the hospital to be with you, pray with you, so you and Stella wouldn't have been alone."

"I should have. I know. I'm not used to having people to rely on for help." Fiona straightened. "I did what I thought was best." Her voice trailed off. "At the time."

Marc plowed his fingers through his hair. "Kidnapping my daughter? Ignoring calls and texts from half of my family?" He shook the hospital report. "Where have you been all this time? The last anyone saw or heard from you was this afternoon."

"The store. The hour's drive to the medical center in Saranac Lake. The doctor's. The hospital for a test." Fiona's voice faltered. "Stella fell asleep. I drove around. I was trying to build up the courage to come home and face you."

"Because your first instinct was to run, like your mother."

Hurt constricted her throat. But in the end, she hadn't fully given in to that instinct as her mother would have. She'd come home with Stella. Fiona cleared her throat. "No, because I love you and Stella, and I know I really messed up."

Fiona's admission of love and her pain drew him to her. But he couldn't touch her, or he'd lose his resolve. "I was scared, too, when I couldn't get a hold of you. I imagined the worst—an accident, losing the people I love most again."

"You love me?" she whispered.

He clenched his fists, so he wouldn't reach over and shake her. Of course he loved her. "I do. But I don't think it's enough for us."

Fiona drew back as if he'd struck her. He reached out and took her hand, rubbing his thumb against her soft skin. "You can't let the past rule you, taking responsibility for everything and micromanaging life into your idea of perfection. God is the only one who's perfect. Not you or me or Pastor Connor. God has a plan for each of us. We have to open our eyes and hearts to that plan."

"I'm trying. The Let Go Meditation with Noah at Bridges."

"I know." He stilled his thumb and squeezed her hand.

"You have to understand. Especially after my stepfather left, I grew up feeling like I was the only responsible person in the house, always in fear of losing my family. Stella's pain, her crying, took me back to that fear and helplessness."

Anxiety tightened her features as if she were reliving

that time, those moments. "We could meet with Noah or Pastor Connor," she said. "I emailed Noah to get together, the three of us, to talk about all the extra time you're throwing into your work. It's been bothering me."

"But you couldn't come directly to me and talk. I admit that the past couple weeks I have been putting in more time at work and spending less time with Stella and you. If you'd said something, I would have recognized it sooner. We can't have a true relationship if you need to keep barriers between us, or if you hide your needs."

His voice cracked, along with his heart. "I know I did that with Cate, imposed my plan on God's plan. I put myself in charge of making us a picture-perfect, up-and-coming young professional family, right down to dictating Cate's treatment against her wishes at the end and closing out my family to deter them from pointing out what I knew deep down. I was fooling myself that my way was God's way."

"How did you stop?"

"Prayer. Lots of prayer. I'm still praying, which obviously I need to be since I didn't pick up that I was putting work ahead of you and Stella." He avoided her gaze so he could finish what he had to say. "And stepping back from the situation. Letting others in to help me with the burden of healing. That's what we need to do, step back from each other."

Fiona nodded. "Stella and your family, too?"

"My family loves you for yourself, whether you and I are a couple or not, and I won't keep Stella from you. You're her aunt."

Fiona pulled her hand from his, taking a piece of his heart with it. "That's all I asked to be." She stood. "I'd better go."

He watched her leave, back straight, steps measured. But he'd come to want more. So much more. And he couldn't help feeling he'd failed Fiona. He'd have to let go himself—of his dreams of him and Fiona and Stella as a family—and think of Fiona as just Stella's aunt, like his sisters. He knew better than to pursue fixing something he couldn't fix again. He'd go it alone. It would be simpler that way.

Chapter Fourteen

I'm not going to make the egg hunt. I have to drive down to Glens Falls. Mom will bring Stella over to the park a little before one. Meet her at the waterfall.

Marc's text made Fiona's heart stumble. True to his word, Marc hadn't kept Stella away from Fiona. He'd kept *himself* away instead.

After nearly a week, an interminably long week, of not seeing or talking or texting with Marc, Fiona had been looking forward to being with him for the Bridges Easter egg hunt as much as she'd been looking forward to the time with Stella. Did the hope that filled her at his trusting her with Stella alone today, and the intense relief that his family wasn't treating her any different, make her pitiful?

Claire was as friendly as always at work. His mother had called one evening and chatted about the plans for Renee's baby shower tomorrow afternoon. She'd even invited Fiona to have Easter dinner with them next Sunday. Fiona had demurred on the dinner, wanting to see how this afternoon's egg hunt with Marc and Stella went.

Now, it was just her and Stella. Fiona admitted to herself that she'd messed things up by not opening up to Marc about her family and her fears earlier—by not trusting Marc and God. Maybe if she could talk with him again. But it didn't look like that would happen today.

She finished her usual Saturday morning chores and headed out into the nippy late March day. While the sunny warm weather last week had melted most of the snow on the ground, today's overcast weather made it chilly enough for a winter jacket and gloves. A few minutes later, Fiona arrived at the park to find Terry and Stella already waiting for her.

"Feena hurry!" Stella shouted when Fiona opened her car door. "Mia's here."

Good. She and Mia's aunt, Kat, could hang out together while the girls hunted for eggs. Kat wasn't Marc, but Fiona had enjoyed talking at the adult Bridges meetings. She should make some friends outside the Delacroix family.

"Hi," Terry said. "I don't know why Marc had to go down to the restaurant this morning."

"It's work. I understand." What Fiona understood was that it was a good excuse for Marc, who was surely not ready to see her again after last week.

"He's fortunate to have you to step in and help with Stella at the last minute when one of the rest of us can't."

Fiona warmed at being included in this way, but hadn't she learned her lesson about expectations? She had what she'd originally wanted, to be Stella's aunt. She should be thankful.

"Come on." Stella slipped her hand in Fiona's.

Fiona shook off her melancholy. She'd leave it up to God to determine the future.

"Do you want me to pick Stella up at three, or do you want to drop her off at the house?" Terry asked before leaving.

"I'll bring her by the house." She was offering so Terry wouldn't have to come into town again, not because she hoped she might run into Marc there—if he was back from the job.

"Bye, Gammy," Stella said, hopping from foot to foot.

Fiona smiled at her niece's excitement. She walked her to the pavilion where the group was meeting, reveling in Stella's lack of sadness at Terry leaving and Fiona stepping in.

"Hey," Kat said when they joined the Bridges group at the pavilion. "No Marc?"

"Daddy work," Stella said before Fiona could answer.

"Should we go around together?" Kat asked. "Noah just said they have a separate hunt set up for the kindergartners and preschoolers, so the bigger kids don't get all the eggs first."

"Good plan." Fiona glanced down at the two little girls.

"Gammy got me a basket," Stella said, lifting the pink-and-yellow basket she held.

"I have my basket, too," Mia said, not to be outdone.

"You girls are ready," Fiona said. "We have to listen now to hear what we're supposed to be doing."

"Finding eggs. Gammy said."

Fiona and Kat laughed at Stella's remark, and Fiona put her finger to her lips, and then to Stella's. "Listen."

The little girl gave her a grin and giggle that made Fiona want to scoop up Stella and hug her.

Noah finished the instructions, and the adults lined the kids up on the left side of the pavilion.

"Ready...set..." Noah blew a whistle to start the hunt.

Stella, Mia and the others raced onto the grass.

"I hope they don't trample all the eggs in their enthusiasm to find them," Kat said.

Fiona laughed. "Me, too."

"Feena, I got one!" Stella shouted, holding it up for Fiona to see.

"Good work," she said.

After the first burst of energy, most of the children slowed down and were searching in the grass, behind rocks and under bushes for the colored plastic eggs.

Kat looked from side to side. "Not many dads here," she observed.

"Marc had planned to be. His work conflict was last minute." Or at least it was to Fiona. She didn't know why she was jumping to his defense when earlier she'd thought he was working to avoid her.

But deep down, she knew why. Because Marc was a good, loving father.

"Oh, I didn't mean Marc. I meant in general." Kat waved her arm at the adults.

"Sadly, I see what you mean. I probably didn't notice because my father never came to things like this." Nor had her mother, much of the time. "And he left when I was eleven." Fiona pressed her fingers to her mouth. What had come over her that she was telling an almost-stranger about her family?

"My dad came to everything," Kat said, "to the point where, when I was older, I wished he didn't." The woman's smile belied her words. "I'm glad he's willing to be there for Mia, too. I just wish he and Mom lived closer."

Fiona braced herself for the wave of jealousy she often felt toward people with loving, intact families. It didn't come. Her heart swelled. She had Stella and the Delacroixs and, at some point, she and Marc might get back to being friends, at least.

After about twenty minutes, Noah blew the whistle again and pronounced the younger kids' hunt finished. The adults rounded them up to have hot chocolate at the pavilion.

"Look, Feena." Stella placed her basket on the ground and squatted. "One, two, free, four, five, five, five." She stopped and looked to Fiona for help.

Fiona could have melted into one of the snow puddles that dotted the park. "Six, seven, eight. You found eight eggs." Fiona gave into her earlier urge and swept Stella into her arms.

"I found eight, too," Mia said proudly.

"Down." Stella pushed against her chest. "Hot choc-it."

Fiona let Stella go and admired Mia's eggs, too, before they walked the girls to a table in the pavilion where a parent volunteer placed a cup of hot chocolate in front of each of them.

"Mmm," Mia said.

"Mmm," Stella copied, a chocolate foam mustache adorning her upper lip.

Fiona pulled a napkin from the dispenser on the table. Before she could wipe Stella's face, the little girl scrambled off the table bench.

"Daddy!" Stella shouted and took off across the park.

She was so quick. Fiona dashed out of the pavilion after her and stopped. Marc could see Stella coming, and there was nothing dangerous between the pavilion and him. She checked the impulse to go after her and watched with bittersweet joy as Stella launched herself into Marc's arms.

Fiona hadn't been jealous earlier when Kat had talked about her family. But seeing Stella with Marc's strong arms holding her close, she was jealous of them both.

"Piggy, Daddy," Stella said after he caught her and swung her into his arms.

Marc lifted his daughter onto his shoulders. He'd hated to miss the egg hunt, but his contractor had called late last night with a minor finishing change he wanted to make today that he insisted needed Marc's in-person approval. His first thought after feeling disappointment was that he had Fiona to cover for him. He pinned his gaze on Fiona standing across the park, waiting for them, and his heart constricted. He wanted Fiona to be there for him always, for more than just Stella.

By midweek, he'd admitted to himself that he'd been overly harsh with her. He'd missed seeing her face, hearing her voice, the anticipation that sprang alive in his gut when his phone pinged with a text that might be from her. He admitted that she'd been genuinely afraid—not that he hadn't been afraid, too, for Stella *and* Fiona. Providing was his strong suit. This nurturing business was still new to him.

If only Fiona had been more open about her family situation, and if he'd only encouraged her when she had shared. He would have had more basis for understanding. He'd figured today, after being together with Stella, would be a perfect time to talk with Fiona. He'd missed the egg hunt, but they still had the rest of the afternoon.

Stella tugged on his ear and he turned his head. "Daddy, swings. I want to swing."

"In a few minutes, sweetpea. You need to show me all the eggs you found." *And I need to convince Fiona to spend the rest of the afternoon with us, and maybe the evening, too.* Playing on the swings should tire Stella out. Then hopefully she'd fall asleep in the car and nap long enough for Fiona to come back to his house so the two of them could talk, see what they could salvage.

Four strides later, they reached the pavilion and Fiona.

"Me and Mia got eight eggs," Stella chattered on. "Feena said I'm good. Right, Feena, I'm a good egg finder?" she asked.

"The best, in my opinion," Fiona said, with a smile that hit him hard in the gut.

Yeah, the best. Only Marc wasn't thinking about eggs.

"Hi." His voice cracked. Marc cleared his throat. "Stella and I thought we'd collect her basket and go swing for a while."

"And she has a prize, too." Fiona lowered her voice. "All the younger children get a stuffed animal." She pointed toward a table. "Stella's things are over there with Kat."

"Wait, aren't you going to stay? Stella. The swings." Marc fumbled with his words, his mind racing to come up with reasons for Fiona to stay.

Fiona's eyes brightened. Or maybe he'd imagined it because it was what he wanted to see.

"No," Stella said. "Feena, eggs. Daddy, swing."

He didn't want to force either Fiona or Stella. Fiona probably had other things to do. But against his better judgment, he cajoled, "It'll be fun to have Fiona with us."

"Feena, egg hunt. Daddy, swing," Stella insisted. "Feena go home."

"Stella! That wasn't nice."

Fiona bit her lip and said softly, "She's tired and

wants time with you. I understand. I'll see you tomorrow at church. Bye, Stella." Fiona started toward the street where her car was parked.

He'd lost his opportunity, or maybe his courage. But he'd see her tomorrow.

"Bye, Feena," Stella called, as if she hadn't just told Fiona to leave, which he was sure she didn't fully realize she'd done.

"Didn't you have fun today with Fiona?" he asked.

"I had fun." Stella nodded so emphatically her ski cap almost fell off. "I like Feena."

"I do, too, sweetpea. I do, too." He walked Stella to the table and watched as Fiona's figure grew smaller in the distance. Adrenaline shot through him. Because of his arrogance that he, and only he, knew what was best for his family, he'd lost his chance for "laters" before with Cate's death. He wasn't going to lose this one. Marc started after Fiona.

"A chickie, Daddy," Stella squealed, pulling him back. "Like at Papa's farm."

When he looked across the park again, the words to ask Kat to watch Stella for a minute on his tongue, Fiona was in her car signaling to pull away from the curb.

Kat handed Stella the stuffed chick from a familiar-looking basket on the table. "It's your prize for finding so many eggs." Kat looked behind Stella and Marc. "Where's Fiona?"

"She had to go." Emptiness filled him. Had he lost his opportunity again?

"We need to head off, too," Kat said.

Stella said goodbye to her friend and snuggled the stuffed chick against her cheek. "No prize for Daddy. Share with me?"

Marc allowed himself a last glimpse across the park

in the direction Fiona had gone and rubbed the soft fabric of the toy. "Thank you, sweetpea."

But he had a prize. He just didn't know how to claim it.

The next afternoon, Fiona stood outside a storage shed on the Delacroix farm with Marc's mother. Spending time with Stella at the egg hunt and seeing Marc had reinforced what Fiona had already thought, even before she'd messed up. She needed and wanted him in her life. The three of them belonged together.

Calling Marc's mother yesterday with the plan that had taken seed in her mind on the drive home had gotten Fiona a surprising reaction.

"I'm glad someone is doing something to put the two of you out of your misery," Terry had said. She had also shared that last Monday, Stella had announced to Andie and the rest of The Kids Place that "Daddy is mad at Feena, but I'm not." Fiona felt her cheeks warm. So the whole family, maybe the whole community, knew.

From what his mother had said, Stella had based her information on a talk Marc had had with her about him and Fiona and Stella not doing things together for a while. Maybe that was why Stella hadn't wanted her to stay and watch her swing.

Terry hadn't pried. She'd simply said, "I don't know what that man has done, but you have my help to fix it. And anytime you need a mother to talk to, you have my number."

Fiona had realized then that she'd gained the family she'd yearned for since her own family had fallen apart. One of her family's downfalls was that they had no sense of community, not in the way she had here—with or without a romantic relationship with Marc. Raising a child was a joint effort. With family, no one person had to take full responsibility.

Fiona crossed her arms and hugged herself against the cold wind that had picked up. *Lord, please guide me in what I'm about to do, that it's Your will and not mine, and help me to accept the outcome, whatever it is.*

"Let's get this going," Marc's mother said. She stepped to the shed door and unlocked it. "You wait inside. As we planned, I called Marc this morning and said I needed him to come and get the crib John and I bought for Renee and Rhys out of the shed and load it in our truck for the shower. I told him that John's shoulder is acting up, and I didn't want him lifting anything heavy." Her voice took on a conspiratorial tone. "I didn't tell him that his father's shoulder acts up every morning."

"He didn't sound suspicious?" Fiona ran her palms down the front of her jeans.

"Nope. But I'd better get back up to the house or he might think something is up. I asked him to be here about ten, and it's five of. Stand behind the barn siding that's leaning against the back wall," Marc's mother directed, "so he doesn't see you when I open the door."

"Okay." Fiona stepped into the shed and listened to Mrs. Delacroix locking the door behind her. *This is it.*

Six minutes later—she knew because she'd checked her phone almost minute by minute—Fiona heard the murmur of voices outside.

"You didn't need to walk down with me, Mom."

She listened for a note of suspicion in his voice.

"Like I said, the lock can be temperamental. There's a trick to getting it to open."

"You could buy a new lock," Marc offered.

"Why, when this one is perfectly good?"

Fiona heard the clatter of Mrs. Delacroix opening the lock. "There," she said, throwing open the door.

Marc walked in and flicked the light switch. "Where..."

His mother closed the door behind him and clicked the lock.

"Is the crib?" he said into the air, before demanding, "What's going on?" and trying the lift latch on the inside of the door.

Fiona stepped out from behind the siding.

"Fiona."

The sound of her name on his lips flowed over her like a cleansing wash. "Marc."

He motioned at the door. "This was your idea?"

"Yes, so we could talk with no distractions." Except the distraction of having him so physically close. It would be so easy to step into his arms, and from his darkening eyes, she didn't think he'd deny her.

"Fiona," he repeated in a raspy voice.

She raised her hand. "Let me talk, and then you can, if you want. If you don't want to, I'll text your mother, she'll unlock the door and I'll accept my place in your family as Stella's aunt and nothing more."

He opened his mouth but didn't speak before he nodded.

"I've prayed. More than I ever have before. I love you and Stella so much. I would never do anything purposely to hurt you. But I know I did by not trusting you, your family or God for help. I'm ready to let go of my past. Take down the barriers."

She paused and pinned his gaze with hers, looking for acceptance in the dark depths. Her pulse quickened when she saw a glimmer of light.

"But I need help. Lots of help. Especially yours."

Marc stared at her as if calculating her words. Then his expression softened with what looked like relief. "You have it—my help, me, everything I am and own. I love you. I've missed you so much this week." He opened his arms. "Come here."

Despite not being finished with everything she wanted to say, Fiona stepped into them, and he held her close, his heart thumping in time with hers.

"This is where you belong, for always."

It took all the strength she had to pull back. She touched her finger to his lips. "Not yet. I haven't finished. You have to let go, too."

He stiffened, making her pulse stutter. But she had to go on. "You have to let go of your need to prove yourself a success."

"You mean my work? Leaving you and Stella at the carnival and at your place after the movie? That was all temporary, part of the start-up. It will calm down once La Table Frais is open."

"Will it? Or is La Table Frais a stepping stone back to being a chef at a New York City restaurant, back to your old life? You did mention going back to New York when we were watching *Frozen* with Stella."

He leaned his forehead against hers. "I said that, didn't I?"

"You did. Do you want to go back to the city?"

"No," he admitted. "I'm happier here, and so is Stella. We need family around us."

"Then stay here. You don't have anything to prove to me or your family—the people who matter. You're a complete man, with or without the outward trappings of success."

"I might want to buy La Table Frais from my partners."

"Let go first, before you do that." She released a wobbly laugh. "If I have to, you have to."

"I'll do my best."

"Don't you always?" she teased.

He lifted her chin so she was looking directly into his eyes. "We're some pair, aren't we?"

"Actually, I think we're two halves of a whole." If she was in this deep, she might as well throw away caution and take the plunge. "You complete me."

"You complete me, too." He lowered his head and captured her lips in a kiss that she felt all the way down to her toes. It made her lose track of time and everything except the safety she felt in his strong arms.

Finally, he drew back. "Although I could stay and do this all day long, I have a crib to load into Dad's truck for Mom."

Fiona blinked his handsome face into focus. "And I have a shower gift to wrap."

"What do we do to get out of here?" he asked.

"I have to text your mother." Fiona tapped in the message.

When she raised her head, he was looking at her with an expression so full of love and caring, Fiona thought her heart would burst.

"Ready?" he asked.

"With you by my side, I'm ready for anything."

"Even my family?"

"Especially *our* family."

Epilogue

That fall

"Do you think Stella will forgive us for making her ride with your parents?"

Marc looked at his beautiful bride of a half hour and slid into the limousine next to her. "She'll get over it, and also having to stay with them this coming week while we're cruising the Caribbean."

"I suppose." Fiona lifted her veil and moved it over her shoulder away from him before rearranging the lace-covered skirt of her gown. "We could have brought her. I read in the cruise line literature that the trip we booked has all kinds of activities for children. 'You won't even know they're there,' one of the brochures said."

"Not know she's with us? This is Stella you're talking about—our very own pipsqueak wedding planner." Marc chuckled, releasing the last of his tension remaining from the whole crazy process leading up to their marriage ceremony at Hazardtown Community Church.

He'd heard people say that their weddings were a blur, but for him, every moment from Fiona appearing at the back of the church on his father's arm was etched in his mind. The ceremony hadn't been perfect. One of the twin's heels had caught in her gown, and she'd stumbled, but her sister caught her. They'd both held their heads high and continued as if nothing had happened. Then his sister Natalie had tied the wedding bands so securely to the pillow Luc carried that his best man, Paul, had had trouble untying the knot to hand him Fiona's ring.

"What's that cat-who-caught-the-canary look on your face for?" Fiona asked.

He nuzzled her cheek. "Are you my canary?"

She playfully pushed his shoulder. "We're in front of the church."

"Relax." He stretched out his legs and squeezed her shoulder. "We're married."

"And in a pretty hasty fashion, according to your grandmother's friend."

"I'm proud of the way you handled that in the reception line." Marc had been ready to leap to her defense when they overheard the woman's comment, but he hadn't needed to.

Fiona shrugged. "She kind of made me feel like I fit in, like I've been accepted as one of the locals if I'm worth talking about."

Unbound love stirred in his heart. They'd both come so far in the past few months. She'd done so much for him, to complete him.

"Besides, all I did was speak the truth. We love each other. Why wait?"

"And it didn't hurt that you have an in with the reception venue manager, so we didn't have to wait months for an open Saturday." He paused. "You don't mind my partners using our reception being held at La Table Frais to advertise the restaurant's banquet facilities?"

She leaned her head on his shoulder. "No. You've been so steadfast at resisting their not-so-subtle hints about revving up your work schedule, maybe opening another restaurant in the Catskills, that I can give in on the advertising."

The limousine driver pulled onto the interstate and cranked up the speed. Marc slid open the window to the front seat. "Take your time," he said.

But all too soon, they were at La Table Frais.

"About time you got here," Paul greeted them at the door to the banquet room. He signaled the DJ.

"And here they are, our bridal couple, Marc and Fiona Delacroix," the DJ boomed into the microphone.

"That's my daddy and mommy!" Stella shouted.

"She called me mommy," Fiona whispered.

Stella hopped off the chair next to his mother and raced over to them.

Marc rested his hand on their daughter's shoulder and studied the profile of the woman he loved with all his heart as she looked into the room at their friends and relatives.

"I'm the most blessed person in the world right now," she said.

Fiona slid her fingers into his and squeezed his hand, the simple sign of affection making him go weak in the knees. He scanned the crowd gathered to help them celebrate their joy and love, ending with her.

"You'll have to settle for second-most blessed."

* * * * *

Dear Reader,

If *A Mom for His Daughter* is the first of my books that you've read, I hope you enjoyed it, and thank you so much for picking it up. I know you have many book options to choose from. If you're one of my regular readers, welcome back to Paradox Lake. I'm sure you recognized some old faces, and I hope you liked meeting the new ones.

As with Marc and Fiona, we'd all like our lives to go a certain way—our way. But often that isn't the best way for us or for those we love. Convincing Fiona and Marc of this wasn't an easy task for me. I hope I did it in a satisfying way for you as a reader.

To keep in touch with me and my new releases, please sign up for my author newsletter at JeanCGordon.com or follow me on Amazon (http://amzn.to/2kVET0w). And feel free to email me at JeanCGordon@gmail.com or snail mail me at PO Box 113, Selkirk, NY 12158. You can also visit me at Facebook.com/JeanCGordon.author or Tweet me at @JeanCGordon.

Blessings,
Jean C. Gordon

Get 2 Free Books,
Plus 2 Free Gifts—
just for trying the Reader Service!

Love Inspired®

LI17R3

SPECIAL EXCERPT FROM

*He'll help fix up her home for her and her four amazing
kids, but after leaving her at the altar years ago,
can Luke Wheeler earn Amish widow Honor King's
forgiveness—and love—once more?*

Read on for a sneak preview of
A MAN FOR HONOR
by ### Emma Miller,
available February 2018 from Love Inspired!

Leaving the cellar door open, Luke came down the stairs
and settled on one of the lower steps. "I suppose Sara is
trying to match us up. It is what she does for a living. And
from what I hear, she knows what she's doing."

Honor pursed her lips, but the look in her eyes didn't
appear to be disapproving.

Luke took it as a positive sign and forged ahead. "I
already know we'd be a good fit. Perfect, in fact, if it
wasn't for what happened last time you agreed to marry
me. We have to talk about it someday," he insisted.

"Maybe, maybe not." She shrugged. "But definitely
not today. I'm having a wonderful time, and I don't want
anything to ruin it."

"Sit with me? Unless you think you'd better go up and
check on the children."

Honor regarded him for a long moment, then lowered
herself onto the step beside him. "*Ne*, I don't want to
check on the children. There are enough pairs of eyes to
watch them and, truthfully, I'm enjoying having someone

else do it." She glanced away and he noticed a slight rosy tint on her cheeks. "Now I've said it," she murmured. "You'll think me a terrible mother."

"I think you're a wonderful mother," he said. "An amazing person who never deserved what I did to you."

Her eyes narrowed. "Didn't we agree we weren't going to discuss this?"

"Not really. You said we weren't. I never agreed. Thinking back, I wonder if we'd just—"

The door at the top of the cellar steps abruptly slammed shut. Then they heard the latch slide into place and the sound of a child's laughter.

Luke got to his feet. "What's going on?" He reached the top of the steps and tried the door. "Locked." He glanced down at Honor. "Sorry."

"Not your fault." She pressed her lips together. "Unless I miss my guess, one of my little troublemakers is at it again."

He chuckled. "When you think about it, it is pretty funny."

She flashed him a smile so full of life and hope that it nearly brought tears to his eyes, a smile he'd been praying for all these years.

Don't miss
A MAN FOR HONOR by Emma Miller,
available February 2018 wherever
Love Inspired® books and ebooks are sold.

www.LoveInspired.com